BOUND

BREAKERS HOCKEY #9

ELISE FABER

BREAKERS HOCKEY SERIES

CHAPTER ONE

Claire

JUST ANOTHER WORK DAY.

Just another pregame snack run.

Or so I tell myself.

I roll my shoulders, trying to ease the ache in my loaded-down arms as I hurry down the hall toward the Breakers locker room. As I brace because I know what I'm about to see.

Who I'm about to see.

Hockey players shouldn't make my heart race.

Not after all this time.

Not after being all but adopted as the team's little sister.

But Jackson does.

They also shouldn't make my blood boil.

I work with these guys on a day-to-day basis. We banter. We tease each other and spend loads of time together during the season. I'm friendly to actual friends with most of them.

Just...not Jackson.

Sighing, I focus on the task at hand—delivering pregame snacks so I can get back to my real duties as assistant to the General Manager of the Breakers hockey team—and shove any thoughts of Jackson down—boiling blood or heart racing or otherwise. I turn into the locker room. I need to be a professional, need to be focused on the job at hand. I need to be…

Not be swooning after a certain hockey player…who I love or hate, depending on the day.

I need to not be—

I screech to a halt in the open doorway, mouth falling open, bag of snacks and Aiden's hot dog nearly slipping from my grasp.

Biting back a gasp, I dash out of the room and turn and press my forehead against the cool wall, eyes slamming closed, cheeks scorching hot, heart racing all over again.

Because holy mother of all the pucks on the ice, I can't *see* these things.

Can't see Jackson Hunter with those chocolate brown eyes and wavy dark hair, the perfect amount of stubble on his face and that body built for sin…

Wearing a pair of tiny, skintight boxer briefs.

Wearing *only* a pair of tiny boxer briefs.

Showing off a body that's…

Well, it's provided sexy fodder for my dreams many a night.

And it likely will again *to*night.

If only he didn't hate me.

My fantasies would be so much better.

"Enough," I whisper, pushing away from the wall and shoving down all of those pesky emotions that Jackson invokes. I have a job to do—I need to check in with Luc and then I have some paperwork to take care of and meetings to schedule and team bonding events to brainstorm.

And most importantly, the guys need their pregame snacks.

The gas station hot dog wrapped in foil paper for Aiden is growing cold in my hand, and I've almost dropped the bag of roasted but unsalted almonds for Marcel at least three times.

Plus, Raph needs his chocolate muffin, and Walker his lemon-lime Gatorade, and—

Jackson needs his peanut butter and strawberry jelly sandwich on boring old white bread.

Eaten exactly forty-two minutes before game time.

And it's forty-*five* minutes before puck drop.

I'm not going to be the reason he has a bad game.

Hockey players and their superstitions.

It's too much.

Or maybe I'm grumpy about it because my heart's racing and my legs are like that jelly, and I know I'm going to be dreaming about Jackson tonight.

Again.

"Focus, woman," I order myself.

If silly foods and rituals are what it takes for the guys to have a good game, then that's what it takes for them to have a good game.

Who am I to judge?

Not to mention, I can make a mean PB & J. And I'm a pro at buying random gas station hot dogs—as barf-inducing as that life skill is. I can keep specific brands of almonds at the ready and eat chocolate muffins alongside Raph—because I always buy one myself from Dommie's bakery...or, okay, fine, I buy myself a couple if I'm feeling really peckish.

(And I'm always feeling peckish).

My job is to help the Breakers be successful, and I take it seriously.

Even if Jackson Hunter makes me want to both run away and lick him like a lollipop.

At the same time.

"Stop delaying," I whisper and straighten my shoulders.

Right. Let's do this.

I step into the locker room—

And nearly swallow my tongue for the second time.

The room isn't empty like my nighttime fantasies—the

ones where Jackson orders me to turn around and settle my hands on the bench, the ones where he takes his time tugging off my pants or lifting my skirt. Where he kicks my legs apart, settles his cock at my entrance, and—

My knees wobble.

Thankfully, that snaps me out of my sex haze, and I wrench my gaze away from Jackson in those truly tiny boxer briefs, the material straining against his muscular thighs, lovingly caressing his pert, biteable ass, the waistband hanging low enough to expose those indents at the top of his hips that I'm desperate to trace my tongue along.

Food. Drinks. Pregame rituals.

That's what I'm here for.

Not a snack of a man.

Not—

"Clairey girl!" Smitty calls from across the room, making me jump and nearly lose the hot dog a second time—something that Aiden notices if him hurrying toward me and snagging it from my hand is any indication.

"Thanks," he murmurs softly, tugging at a lock of my hair.

"Of course," I tell him, tossing a smile in his direction that's fake as hell before hurrying to the table I set up on the far side of the room earlier.

"You good?" Smitty booms—because the big defenseman never just talks, he booms, his voice echoing across the room, filling up all available space...except with his woman.

She's the opposite of him—soft-spoken and shy—and Smitty is different with her.

A big teddy bear.

Almost quiet.

Definitely gentle.

I can't lie. I'm jealous of that gentle he gives Kailey.

My life hasn't—

No.

"I'm good!" I call back, clinging to the make-believe that

I'm fine, that I'm completely unaffected by the man who plea-sures me in my dreams and glares at me in real life. "Just working my way through my mental check list as usual," I say lightly, tossing Smitty his pregame snack of choice—a pack of Sour Patch Kids—then tapping my temple with now free hand. "It's quite long today."

He smiles at me—the warm, Smitty smile that won me over years ago now, that made me trust, that helped me open my heart enough to trust him and the others.

I would do anything for him.

Anything for *all* of them.

Which is why Jackson can't stand me.

"Always a million miles ahead, aren't you?"

Unbidden, my gaze swivels to Jackson, who's come close enough that my stomach flutters, my body wants to sway forward, to feel all the strength of him against the softness of me.

"No," I say quietly, "but I try."

That makes him scowl, to unleash the familiar glare in my direction.

"Here's your sandwich," I tell him, shoving it at him and forcing a smile as I turn to the table and start unloading my bag and the rest of the goodies, double-checking that everyone has what they need to play the best hockey they can play.

"You coming on the next road trip?" Smitty asks.

Now my smile is genuine. "I wouldn't miss New York for anything."

The bright lights, the bustling city. Central Park. Food that makes my mouth water just thinking about it. Bakeries and Broadway shows.

So full of life when mine...

Isn't.

Or wasn't.

Things are different now.

I'm not alone. I have friends and—

Jackson snorts and I clench my back teeth together, ignore the bolt of pain cascading through my jaw, then turn for the door.

"Wait," he mutters, reaching out as though to take my arm.

I skitter back.

He clenches his hand into a fist, and he drops it to his side.

There might be regret on his face, might be a thousand other emotions trailing through his deep brown eyes.

But I don't get the chance to see them.

Because just as quickly as he started to stop me...

He's turning away.

Only...why do I get the sense that he's *running* away?

CHAPTER TWO

Jackson

The fucking sandwich tastes like sawdust.

Not simple carbs and fast-acting sugars and a dash of protein to sustain my blood sugar.

Eaten exactly forty-two minutes before the game.

Part superstition. Part necessity.

I work my ass off on the ice.

I can't have my glucose levels crashing as I'm trying to chase down a puck or sprinting down the ice on a breakaway or battling on the boards so the fuckers on the other team don't get a free shot at our goalie.

But my normal pregame snack tastes like shit.

And I know it's because of Claire.

Because of how I am with Claire.

A dick.

Sighing, I shove the rest of the sandwich in my mouth, forcing myself to chew and swallow, to eat the snack I don't really want, that I'm not hungry for. Not the first time and it won't be the last. My blood sugar doesn't always play nicely with the contents of my stomach. But I know that I'm going to need it.

So, I make myself choke it down.

Bite, chew, swallow.

And repeat until I finish it.

But I'm still cursing my asshole of a pancreas.

Could ya just produce some insulin so I don't have to waste a good chunk of my brain power at all times trying to sustain my blood sugar and can instead focus on other shit?

Like hockey like the rest of the guys.

Like points and checks and maintaining a good plus-minus.

Like—

I sigh.

For better or worse, that's not my life.

Brushing the crumbs off the tips of my fingers, I pull on my gear.

It doesn't take long. Undergarments, pads, socks, skates. Hockey pants, jersey, helmet. A glance at my phone, checking my levels, making sure nothing fucked-up is happening. If my blood sugar is too high, it can fuck up my eyes, my heart, my nerves, my kidneys, my blood vessels—fun right? And too low, and I can pass out, have a seizure, hit my head.

Oh, or die.

That's a fun fact.

Today, though, my numbers are behaving and I'm good to shove on my gloves, snag my stick from the rack by the door.

Warm-up.

Sit and wait as the crowd files in.

Then game time.

And getting a fucking win against the Grizzlies—the newest team in the league and pretty much the biggest pains in the asses to play against.

I never thought the Sierra would give up that mantle.

But they sure as shit have.

The Grizzlies are a motley crew of old guys and rookies, and they're tenacious as fuck with a renegade head coach who's blasting through barriers left and right.

A former Olympian. A gold medalist many times over. A scout, a skating coach, an assistant and now…the first female head coach in the league.

Kick ass for sure.

But, God, I hate playing against her team.

Rolling my shoulders, I step out onto the ice, glancing up at the rapidly filling arena, our fans in Breakers blue and the jagged pieces inside me settle.

This is where I feel myself, where I feel normal, where I can just be a player and not someone with a disability, with a life-long illness that requires constant management. Where I'm not the kid who was teased by my teammates and classmates about eating too much sugar or junk food—newsflash, that's not how someone gets diabetes. Where I don't feel awkward and exposed because my medical devices are beeping or I'm surreptitiously pounding fast-acting carbs or my stomach hurts because my numbers are off.

It's been years since a teammate—and definitely longer since a classmate—has been a dick about me having type one, but that shit sticks deep.

So, even now, stepping onto the ice feels like a weight has been lifted from my shoulders.

Today's about pucks and hitting hard and connecting passes and winning against the fucking Grizzlies.

"Let's fucking go, yeah?" Smitty says—or yells, basically, because the man has never met an inside voice that he likes. He claps a big hand on my shoulder as he zips by me with a speed that belies his size, scooping up a puck and focusing on his own pregame routine.

I skate and stretch, my muscles warm already from the thirty minutes on the bike I did before getting dressed, but I still take a moment to stretch, to check in with my body, to loosen up my hands and wrists.

To focus.

And I'm ready by the time the buzzer counts down and we slip off the ice, marching down the hall to swap out our practice jerseys for the game ones, to plunk our gloves on the drier, to change out any equipment that's uncomfortable—or needs to be swapped for the lucky version, e.g. Aiden and his lucky T-shirt with the Superman emblem he wears during every game.

Coach comes in and gives his pregame check in and pep talk.

Marcel always has something insightful to say.

Smitty cracks jokes.

And I'm here, in this moment...

At least until my phone beeps, interrupting the punchline.

I grit my teeth together, make the necessary adjustments on my pump, eat a couple of spoonfuls of peanut butter from the jar that's in my cubby—a jar that I know Claire put there because she's thoughtful and beautiful and far too fucking good for my ass, even though I've wanted to fuck her from almost the first moment I saw her, all those years ago, and wanted to claim her as my own the more I've gotten to know her. Thoughtful. Gorgeous. A survivor with a backbone that rivals any of the guys in the locker room.

She's fucking *everything*.

Just not for me.

I toss the plastic spoon in the trash, screw the lid on the peanut butter and stow it back onto the shelf.

One more numbers check and then I'm giving my phone to the trainer, Sam, so she can keep one eye on my numbers while I'm playing.

She has low sugar snacks on her at all times during practices and games, and I'll sip from a bottle filled with Gatorade as needed, but the adrenaline should kick in soon and between that and the peanut butter and my sammy, I'll be good.

I always am.

Always find a way to make it through—even when the odds are against me.

Thankfully, as I'm taking care of this shit, Smitty doesn't stop with the jokes, keeping the locker room loose and relaxed, and by the time we're all lined up and filing down the hall, the team's entrance song on blast, the stadium full, I'm focused again.

I'm ready to play hockey.

Ready to grind out a win, to feel the cool air on my cheeks as I skate hard, to hear the crunch of my blades on the ice, the back-and-forth chirping from my teammates and the assholes on the other bench. I'm ready to work my ass off and do what I love.

Claire's standing in the hall, just inside the entrance.

And suddenly, my focus is off.

It's back to yearning and claiming and knowing…

I can't have her.

I'm no good for her.

I'm not enough for her.

But I still want to pull her close and taste her anyway.

CHAPTER THREE

Claire

I'm watching the game against the Grizzlies from Luc's suite situated high above the ice…

And it's not going well.

Okay, the team is doing fine—it's just that Jackson isn't.

He's…off.

That's the only way I can describe the passes he's missed—including one that would have gotten the team and him an easy goal—and the trouble he's had getting the puck out of his own zone, the clear frustration on his face at the end of his shifts. And, frankly, he's sitting on the bench more tonight than he's been skating on the ice.

At least this period.

Damn.

It's not his blood sugar.

Not right now, anyway.

His number has been steady since the puck dropped—this according to Sam and my nosy self making sure his graph from his continuous glucose monitor is in the safe range—so it's not diabetes.

Not today, anyway.

But something's seriously off.

"I haven't seen him like this since his rookie season," Luc mutters from next to me, and one glance and I can tell he's doing his best to keep his expression neutral.

I'm doing the same—Luc taught me embrace my inner Stone Face, because one never knows when the camera may be panning this direction.

No need being caught on a feed somewhere looking unhappy.

That's just fodder for the sports and gossip blogs.

At least make them work for their stories.

Or work for the Breakers, I think, allowing my mouth to tip up just slightly at the edges, gaze drifting to the box where former sports blogger, Eva Moreno, is broadcasting, now a significant part of the team's television crew.

Luc's sneaky, working his magic on parts of the team that don't necessarily fall under his purview, but that benefit this family he's built.

And I'm soaking in every sneaky moment.

"I don't think I've *ever* seen him like this," I say quietly.

Luc sighs and leans back in his seat, fingers steepled in front of him. "Everyone has an off night."

Not Jackson.

If I've learned anything in the years since I joined the team, way back when Jackson was that rookie, it's that all players have ups and downs.

Except Jackson.

He's the steady on the roster—the guy who always shows up ready to go, whose constant, even energy keeps propelling the team forward, whose calm presence has guided the team to several Stanley Cups.

But that's not the Jackson I'm seeing on the ice tonight.

"Christ," Luc mutters and I jerk, focusing on the rink below, on the sight that has even my Master of the Stone Face boss wincing.

Jackson has launched himself at the biggest guy on the ice, and they've lost their gloves, grabbed on to each other's jerseys, and are punching each other.

Repeatedly.

"Damn," I whisper when Jackson takes a fist to the jaw, sending his head snapping backward and blood gushing down his face. "That has to hurt."

"It does," Luc says. "Even in that moment"—a nod to the ice—"but especially later."

I bite my lip as Jackson takes another blow, even as he unloads several of his own in quick succession. "His face or his hands?" I ask quietly.

"Both." Luc flicks his gaze in my direction. "And everywhere else. It's hard work to fight and that shit strains muscles below muscles that we never knew we had. He'll feel like a truck ran him over tonight—"

"Men and their little games."

He grins, a flash of a smile that's absolutely stunning, and turns in a flash. I'm doing the same because I recognize the female voice, because I know that Luc's wife, Lexi, is standing there. She strolls through the suite and plunks herself into Luc's lap, wrapping her arms around his shoulders and planting a kiss on his mouth so scorching hot that I look away to give them privacy.

Lexi doesn't give a fuck about fodder for gossip blogs.

She's happy and in love and doesn't care who knows it.

My belly twinges with jealousy, but I push that down. She and Luc deserve every bit of happiness.

God knows they deserve it.

I stare down at the ice below again, see that the refs have intervened and separated Jackson from the huge ass player he's been fighting, guiding them to the doors that lead off the ice.

The Breakers are up by three goals, there's less than three minutes left in the game, and Jackson and the other guy will each have at least a five minute penalty for fighting (and likely, Jackson will get extra time because he's the one who started the trouble), so they might as well head to the locker room to get undressed.

Yes, epic comebacks have happened in hockey—*do* happen in this sport where fans should never leave until the final buzzer goes.

But I highly doubt that my guys are going to give up a game they've had in hand since early in the first period.

Not *my* guys.

I still stay in my seat, focusing on the game until the final seconds ticks down, making small talk with Lexi—and hearing some hilarious stories about their son, Noah and his adventures with their new puppy.

"I'll see you tomorrow," Luc says as the guys file off the ice and he packs up his stuff. "But not before—"

"Noon," I finish for him, earning a tug of the end of my ponytail.

"Exactly. Noon and—"

"—not a second earlier," I finish again.

"Smart ass," he mock grumbles then fixes me with a look as he slings his bag over his shoulder.

"I'm just saying that I've learned from the best."

Lexi grins and takes his arm. "Damn right you did." A wink at me. "Because I know you mean *me* and not him."

"Hey!" Luc begins, but she's already drawing him from the room, waving at me, allowing the door to slide closed behind them.

Noon tomorrow.

And not a second before.

I bite back a sigh.

Because what the hell am I going to do for the next twelve-plus hours? Sit silently in my apartment and stare at the walls?

There's no real set hours when someone works for a sports team—we have late nights interspersed with early mornings, flights and bus rides to and from airports and hotels. Practices and games and community outreach events. I could let it be my entire life, if I wanted.

Like I've been known to do in the past.

Which is why I know I earned that gentle admonishment from Luc about noon—and not a second before.

He wants me to have a life that isn't work, that's balanced, that's not just living and breathing the team and my job.

The only thing is…that's fucking hard.

Luc has a family, kids, a dog, a beautiful, happy wife.

He has things to go home to.

I have…an empty apartment and—

"Enough," I whisper, grabbing my purse and slipping from the room.

I have *all* the streaming services. My apartment may be sans kids and family members, but I have plenty of trash TV to watch.

So, my apartment won't be completely empty.

Just absent of anyone but reality TV personalities yelling through the screen.

Sighing, I make my way down to the elevator. I need to stop by my office, get my coat and maybe my laptop—because while Luc said I couldn't come in before noon, he *didn't* say I can't work between now and then.

Grinning, because I love my job and all the things that come with it, I zip out of the elevator doors and—

Promptly slam into a big, strong body.

Into *Jackson's* big, strong body.

CHAPTER FOUR

Jackson

My hands come up to steady her without really thinking, gripping the tops of her shoulders so she doesn't bounce backward and hurt herself.

But the moment my palms make contact with her arms, I'm shocked by how slender she is, how delicate her bones feel beneath my hands.

I could hurt her.

I could touch her wrong, hold her too tightly.

I could *hurt* her.

Like I hurt the asshole on the other team tonight.

Like I—

The memory slices up through me so quickly that I can't block it, can't shove it down like I would normally do. It wraps a hand around my insides, grips tightly, and I drop my hands, jerking back a step.

A sliver of hurt crosses her face.

Shit.

I open my mouth to apologize but then my eyes catch on my knuckles, scraped and bruised and—

Shit.

I skitter back another pace.

"Jackson?" she asks quietly, her voice stroking along my insides, making me want all the things I can't ever allow myself to have.

"Just go," I say gruffly.

"I—" More hurt on her beautiful face before she stifles it, lifts her chin, and says tersely, "Right."

But instead of seeing her turn for the exit of the arena, the one that will dump her out into the employee parking lot, she just spins on her heel and starts down the hallway that leads to her office.

It's after eleven and I know she's been here all day.

Just like I know she works too fucking much and too fucking hard and Luc has made it clear she needs to stop that shit.

"What the fuck are you doing?" I growl, starting after her.

She scowls at me, shakes her head, then keeps walking away from me.

And instead of letting her go—which I fucking *know* is the right thing to do—I go after her, snagging her arm, drawing her to a stop. "I know Luc's talked to you about working too much," I mutter.

"What I do with my life is none of your business," she snaps, jerking free of my hold.

That's loose.

Because I could hurt her.

Exhaling, I shove that down, *way* the fuck down, and focus on controlling my temper.

"Killing yourself for the team isn't what we do here." It's all about work-life balance, coming together, looking after one another, focusing on the fact that a rising tide lifting all boats.

Fucking weird and kumbaya from the outside, but something that makes perfect sense when you're in the fold.

"And what I do with my personal time isn't your business."

"Luc might have something to say about that," I mutter.

Her eyes flare with frustration, but there's a thread of guilt there.

She knows I'm right.

And that needles at me, at the truth she discovered, the reason we've entered into this adversarial relationship in the first place.

"You know I'm right," I press.

She grinds her teeth together and tosses her head, sending the sleek blond strands of her hair sailing through the air like a golden cape. "I *know* that I don't owe you an explanation of my life."

"You're avoiding the truth."

"No," she snaps. "Because the truth is that. My. Life. Is. None. Of. Your. Business."

"This team is my business," I grit out, temper flaring. Why won't she just admit that she's wrong? "Which means you are too."

"Oh," she says archly, "so you're changing your story now?"

I frown. "What the fuck are you talking about?"

"You made it very clear that you see me as nothing more than a lowly intern, a pathetic assistant, a woman who's qualified to make your sandwiches and nothing more."

I blink. Once. Then again. "What the fuck?"

But she doesn't hear me because she's already striding down the hall, turning the corner, and disappearing from sight.

Maybe I shouldn't go after her, but...

Fuck it.

How do I listen to her spout that bullshit and just...watch her walk away?

I catch up with her as she pushes into her office.

"What the fuck?" I ask again.

She makes an adorable fucking squeaking sound I've never heard before, and clamps her hand to her chest, and I want to scare her all over again, just to hear it a second time.

To have that small part of her.

The glimpse of Claire the rest of the world doesn't readily see.

But it's already gone as she snatches her laptop out of the cradle on her desk, starts unplugging cords, and snarks, "Did I stutter?"

My temper flares again and I grind my teeth together, keeping it in check.

Just barely.

"Fucking *sandwiches?*" I growl.

Her gaze flicks to mine and then away as she shoves her laptop into the huge purse she always lugs around. It's practically half her size and looks like it weighs a hundred pounds.

It probably fucking does, considering that she keeps the keys to the kingdom in there.

Snacks and spreadsheets, her ever-present notebook and pen to take notes. And the fucking laptop she's cramming in there.

Working.

Always fucking working.

She doesn't acknowledge me further, though, just grabs the handles of her purse and slings it onto her shoulder—

Or tries to.

Because I snag it from her before she can, and—Christ—the fucking bag *does* weigh a ton. "What do you have in here?" I mutter. "Bricks?"

"No," she grumbles, reaching for it, "I have *sandwiches.*"

A curl of amusement slides through my stomach, but my

annoyance definitely outweighs any humor of this situation. "I don't think of you as someone who just makes sandwiches."

She snorts and grabs her coat, wrenching it off the back of her chair. "Right." She lifts her hand. "Give me my bag please."

"Claire—"

She stills, eyes closing for a second, then exhales opening them and holding my stare. "I can't do this tonight."

"You started it."

"You don't like me," she says quietly. "You've made that clear."

I like her, have liked her far too much from the first moment I saw her. She just...

Knows too much.

"It's not like that."

Her brows flick up, but instead of snapping at me, she rubs her forehead, as though there's a throb beneath the surface. "Then what's it like, Jackson? Because you spend pretty much every moment we're together"—she waves a hand in my direction—"looking at me like that."

"Like what?"

"Scowling," she snaps. "Looking down your nose at me like I'm dog poop on the bottom of your shoe."

"Okay, that's fucking ridiculous."

"Ridiculous?" She laughs, but it's not filled with humor. "Right. Dumb little blond girl who knows nothing. Keep up the gaslighting, Jackson, but do it by yourself." She starts for the hall.

I let her go for a second.

Then I go after her, shutting her office door behind me, trailing her through the hallways, knowing that she'll realize I'm following sooner or later.

She pushes out into the parking lot, not fazed by the cold winter air slamming into me, sinking into my bones like I've been dunked into icy water. I have to force my feet to keep moving, to trail her across the enclosed space, and I reach her just as she's stopped next to her car.

Which is why I see her shoulders slump in resignation when I get near, see the temper leave her as she spins around to face me.

"My bag," she says, holding out a hand.

"You're a lot more than sandwiches and snacks, Claire."

"Right," she mutters, not quite looking at me.

Giving in to the urge that eats at my insides, I gently cup her jaw, tilt her head up so her gaze meets mine. "You're smart and a valuable asset to the team."

"But"—her throat works—"you don't like me."

I reach for the driver's side door, tug the handle, hearing the locks disengage. Then pull it again, opening the metal panel before bending and settling the bag in the passenger's seat. "In the car, Claire," I order softly as I straighten and step back.

"Jackson," she presses, not moving.

I exhale, knowing that I can't have her looking at me like that, can't have her thinking what's she's thinking. "It's not that I don't like you." I suck in a breath, release it. "I just... don't like what you did."

Guilt on her face again, and I feel like an asshole all over again.

I don't like what she found.

Don't like what it says about me.

Don't like that it can ruin me.

But *I* did it, not her.

And I'm a jerk for—

"But you're a good person," I blurt, sending her gaze that had slipped away jerking back to mine.

So much better than me.

"And the guys and I are lucky to have you."

Her mouth falls open.

I nudge her into the car before she can say anything else,

before I can process the expression on her face softening, before I can let it affect me.

Keep her pissed.

Keep her distant.

Keep her safe.

And...keep the demons locked up.

CHAPTER FIVE

Claire

"When are you going to stop working so hard and start giving me some grandbabies?"

I roll my eyes as I set the mug of tea in front of my adopted grandmother. "Technically," I say, pressing a kiss to her cheek, "they'd be great grandbabies, Gran."

She wrinkles her nose. "That makes me sound old."

I sink into the armchair across from her. "That's because you are old."

Scowling, she leans forward and picks up the mug, blowing on the steaming liquid. "Don't remind me." Then she grins, and all teasing about grandbabies is put away. "How is work going, baby girl?"

I sigh in relief.

Gran can be a dog to a bone sometimes—and especially about my future.

She wants me settled down, taken care of.

Because she's getting—the aforementioned—older.

I want that too—a home, a family, kids, maybe an adorable pup or a mischievous kitten. But, most of all, I want a partner who'll love me for who I am inside.

Only…

I can't seem to find one.

Even though I'm surrounded by men on a daily basis.

Jackson in tiny boxer briefs. Jackson carrying my bag. Jackson touching my chin. Jackson saying I'm a good person.

Jackson jumping back when he steadied me. Jackson scowling at me. Jackson finding out that I—

"Claire?"

Shaking myself, I plaster a smile on my face as I replay the conversation and try to remember what the hell she asked me. "Work's going great," I manage to supply. "Luc is really happy with what I've been doing, and the guys are awesome as always."

Gran lifts her mug in salute. "I knew it wouldn't take long for you to get that place into shape. Smartest thing Luc ever did was to promote you."

Truthfully, it hadn't taken much. The Breakers have had my back from the beginning, and they've given me way more than I've given them. Yeah, they're a professional hockey team in the business of winning hockey games, but they are a family first. And they've been that way for far longer than I've been around. I just…

Found my place, knew it was a good one, and did everything I could to stick around.

From intern to social media consultant to assistant to the GM.

I'll take that climb.

And along the way, I finessed the small details, learned all I could about what made the guys tick and how I could help them do well on the ice, how I could adjust all of the moving parts so that the Breakers are the best they can be.

I've tried to make myself indispensable.

But they don't need me, not really. They were fine without me, would be fine if I left.

That's just facts.

But not facts I share with Gran.

I won't add to her worry about me.

She's been doing far too much of that for far long enough.

Taking care of me, stepping up when she didn't have to, making sure I was fed and clothed and safe...and had birthdays and Christmases and summer barbecues and all the things I missed out on while growing up with deadbeats for parents.

I've long been able to stand on my own two feet, but I can see the strain those years wrought on her face, in the deep lines around her mouth and eyes, the dark circles beneath her lower lashes, the paleness of her skin. She's tired, and even though I've barely been here an hour and we've just sat and chatted, these visits are hard on her.

Everything is hard on her nowadays.

Because she is old and though she's a warrior who's beaten cancer twice, the battles sucked a lot of life out of her. She's still my Gran, of course. Just...the spritely Energizer Bunny who played volleyball with me in the back yard when I wanted to try out for the team in junior high, who never met a midnight showing for a movie premiere she didn't love is... changed.

Naps and resting are broken up by short bursts of activity —walking around the block, bringing in packages, reheating the meals I cook for her, gabbing with her girlfriends on the phone, sitting in her chair across from me and talking about our days.

My Gran...but not.

It doesn't matter.

She stepped up to take care of me. There's no way I'm not going to do the same for her.

That's that.

"Tell me how Junie's doing," I order softly as I settle back with my own tea. "Did she get the bingo debacle sorted?"

Bingo is a Big Deal in Gran's circle—yup, with those capital letters—and the debacle with her best friend, June, involved a faulty mic, several intensely frustrated Boomers, and a slice of cake the local pet charity sells at their weekly Bingo Nights getting crushed into someone's face.

Good times in the multipurpose room.

Gran rolls her eyes. "Junie's shirt is ruined from the mix of dabber ink and frosting"—she ended up worse for wear trying to play referee—"but otherwise everything else is resolved and happy and they're not getting kicked out of the school's multi-purpose room after all."

Bingo is WILD.

"That's good news."

"Considering how much work Junie puts into the events," Gran agrees, "it certainly is."

"Did you want me to take you next week?" I ask, knowing that used to be one of Gran's favorite things. "We can play a couple of games, eat a slice of cake"—I feign a casual shrug—"or we could have some fun and ruin another one of Junie's shirts."

Gran's face lights up for a second. But only for a second before that happiness fades. "No," she says. "I'll get too tired and—" She puts down her tea, shakes her head. "No, honey. Thanks for offering but it won't work out."

"Junie could save you a spot by the exit," I tell her. Because it's true. Because Junie is her ride and die and just as much of a mother figure as Gran is in my life. "We could go for a bit, head out if you get tired—"

"No, sweetheart," she says. "Thank you, but no."

"It wouldn't be too much trouble at all. I'm not working that night." The Breakers have an off night in their jam-packed schedule leading toward the back half of the season. "I can just—"

"That's okay, honey."

"Really, though." I know I'm pushing, but I can't help it. I want her to have fun. She hasn't had much of that over the last few years. "I don't mind."

"Another time," she says. "Now tell me—"

"But—"

"Claire!" she snaps. "Just stop."

I flinch at the sharp tone, nearly spilling my tea on myself. Gran rarely raises her voice and even more rarely speaks to me like that. I push down the hurt, know that it's my fault for being a pushy ahole.

How many times had she said no nicely?

Exhaling, I set my mug down. "I'm sorry."

"No," she says, reaching across the table and taking my hand. "*I'm* sorry."

I shake my head. "I was being pushy."

Her mouth ticks up. "And who was responsible for teaching you your pushy skills, my darling girl?"

Lightness in my belly, pushing out the guilt. "I prefer to think of it as you taught me have to a backbone, Gran."

A soft laugh, her fingers tightening around mine. "My wonderful girl."

My heart squeezes as she pulls back and picks up her mug again.

"I have ice cream in the freezer," she says, a familiar mischievous twinkle in her eyes.

I exhale in relief then force my tone to be light. "Wheel of Fortune and empty calories?"

"Is there anything better?"

No.

No, there isn't.

There's nothing better than sitting with the only person in the world who knows every part of me while guessing word puzzles and consuming copious amounts of empty calories.

Nothing.

"I'll dish us up some."

She shakes her head, pushes up to her feet with a wince and a groan, starts tottering toward the kitchen.

"We're going full cartons tonight, baby girl. I'll get them. You get the spoons."

CHAPTER SIX

Jackson

"One more," Smitty says, and it's quiet for him.

But it's still loud enough to make me want to punch him.

I didn't sleep well the last few nights—not with so much to rehash, to replay in my mind.

The shitshow of a game, the stuff with Claire.

I *touched* her.

Fuck, and since then I've dreamed about the softness of her skin, the plumpness of her lips, how easy it would be to taste her.

So fucking stupid.

I should have left her thinking I despised her, that I only think she's good for snacks and sandwiches.

Instead, I blurred lines.

And I can't have that.

"Dude," Smitty says, snagging the bar when I go to press it overhead, "I only said one more."

I let him have the bar, watch as he reracks it, and realize that my arms are shaking, my muscles burned out.

How many extra reps had I done without processing them?

Enough that I'm glad Smitty is here to spot me and make sure I don't end up with a face full of barbell.

"Thanks," I mutter.

"You need to get your shit together, man." His expression is hard—an unusual look on my teammate's face. He's loud and always cracking jokes, there and ready to lighten the moment.

Unless you do something that hurts someone he cares about.

Doesn't matter if the hurting is self-imposed or otherwise— he'll go ham on your ass.

"I need a snack," I mutter before he can unleash the lunch meat, pushing off the bench and winding my way through the weight room before he can start in on me.

But when I push into the player's lounge, it's not to find any relief.

Claire is standing in front of the fridge, a plastic crate of drinks on the floor in front of her.

Restocking.

Always taking care of us.

She glances up...and—

Fuck.

That's enough.

To remind me, to slap me back into place.

This team takes care of each other. *I* need to do the same.

Which means keeping my fucking hands to myself when she looks at me like that—softened on the edges, open and vulnerable. I could take from her. I could find a way to have her.

To have everything from her.

But that's not good for *her.*

I'm not good for her.

I need to erase that softness, need to make it go away and never come back. Need to make sure she stays the fuck away from me—which she should fucking know because she *knows* but—

Just like Smitty, Claire would give anything for the team.

Long hours, overtime, road trips, going above and beyond constantly—

And bending over backward for a man who doesn't fucking deserve it.

Which is why I know I *have* to do it.

Be a fucking dick so she stays the fuck away.

"Hey," she says quietly.

I grunt, move toward her, ignoring the gentle in her eyes, stifling the urge to touch, to inhale deeply, to bind the scent of her to my soul.

"How are—?"

I step deliberately in front of her to reach into the fridge, cutting off her words. I grab a cold bottled drink—cold because she always rotates the bottles, making sure the warm shit's in the back—and turn away.

But not before fucking with the bottles, messing them up.

Because I'm a fucking dick.

Her outraged inhale slices no more deeply than I deserve.

"Are you kidding me?"

I shrug, nudge the plastic bin with my foot, knocking over the bottles in there for good measure.

Dick 2.0.

"Seriously?" she snaps.

I just crack the bottle open, drop the lid onto the counter—and not in the trash can.

"Are you really acting like this?" she grinds out.

"What do you think?"

"I think," she drawls, "that you're a prickly manchild who was nice to me for a second and then panicked that you might have actually acted like a human being and let someone in for a second."

Dread gathers between my shoulder blades.

"And I *think* that now you're back to being a jerk because heaven forbid someone think something nice about you, Jackson Hunter."

I can see it in her face, imagine her words before she even allows them to dance off the tip of her tongue.

Fuck.

"I know," she says. "Yes, I stumbled upon information I shouldn't have had access to, and I know I should have kept my fucking mouth closed and not mentioned it to you that I did. But—"

"Don't," I growl.

"—all of that being said doesn't mean—"

"Don't."

"That you're a bad person."

I move to her in a rush, the sports drink—in a flavor I fucking hate, by the way, something I see her notice, because Claire keeps track of those fucking small details all the time. Plus, it's full sugar, so I can't even drink it without insulin. I'm really fucking this up, especially as it spills out of the open lid, sloshing down the sides, and covering my hand.

Sticky, it already feels sticky.

Like the memories eating me up from the inside.

"Don't," I say again, plunking the bottle on the counter and bending and putting my face in hers, blatantly trying to intimidate her.

And knowing it's not working in the least when she just rolls her eyes, mouth tipped up at the edges.

She's seen through me.

Fuck.

"You're not even that good at being a dick, Jackson," she says. "I'm realizing that now."

"I'm totally a dick." I narrow my eyes. "And I'm good at *everything* I do."

Her mouth ticks up. "Sure you are."

I glare. "You're just a nosy little girl who doesn't know when to mind her own business."

I expect her face to cloud with hurt, expect her eyes to show that same pain from the other night when she was talking about me only seeing her for snacks and sandwiches.

But I don't see it today.

I've given away too much.

"Don't you have to make a snack run?" I ask sarcastically.

"Nope," she says tartly, shoving by me and moving toward the refrigerator. "I have to reorganize this fridge because someone is trying to be a jerk and only mildly succeeding."

Ignoring that, I grab her arm, drag her back toward me. "Why are you so quiet and shy with everyone else"—except Smitty, who has a way of getting anyone to talk—"but such a pain in the ass with me?"

Her mouth flattens out. "I was kind of thinking it was the other way around."

"Hilarious," I mutter.

"Yeah, there's a lot of hilarity going around," she says dryly, reaching for the bottle and capping it.

I narrow my eyes.

She lifts her chin. "You don't even like that kind."

"I do too."

Fucking liar. Fucking child. Fucking moron.

A roll of her eyes. "I'll take it home with me," she says like she's talking to a toddler, probably because...I'm acting like a toddler. "Unlike you, I *do* like it."

"I—"

"Look," she says with an annoyed sigh. "Just stop. We don't have to be best friends, but we do need to get along."

"Did you think that before or after prying into my private life?"

"I didn't mean to—"

I lean closer, near enough to see the specks of gold in her

soft brown eyes. "Pry into sealed files you had no business accessing?"

Guilt on her face. "I—"

There's a clatter behind us and we both whip around—

To see fucking Walker standing across the room, clearly snooping, clearly gathering intel for the Breakers' gossip train, clearly being a fucking pain in my motherfucking ass.

He flicks up his brows, tilts his head toward the hall that leads down to the weight room, silently reminding me that I'm playing with fire.

Christ.

Claire plunks a hand on my chest, shoves me back. "Enough," she hisses.

I freeze, the touch burning through me, but before I can react to it, she slips away from me and hurries from the room.

With the fucking bottle of sports drink clenched in her hand.

CHAPTER SEVEN

Claire

I get tired of staring at the walls in my empty apartment.

My earlier visit with Gran this afternoon was cut short when she fell asleep on the couch, so I covered her up, made sure her fridge was stocked, that she had snacks and drinks within arm's reach and then went home.

To stare at those walls.

Until the quiet becomes overwhelming and I find myself getting in my car and driving…

To CeCe's.

It's just a local bar and restaurant—nothing fancy—but the food is good, the music is great, and the back room feels like a secret hideaway for just me and the crew from the Breakers.

"Claire!"

Case in point?

Several of the guys are taking up most of a large round table on the far side of the room. They wave me over, and I can't lie, I feel a wave of relief when I see Raph, Walker, Cas, and Smitty…and no Jackson.

The scene in the player's lounge a few days ago has been imprinted on my mind.

Jackson's body.

The heat in his eyes and how it stoked the embers of need in my belly, always present when he's near, but transformed into flames that threaten to incinerate me when he was so close to me, so focused on me, so...*much* to me.

And when he touched me, when his body came close, when I felt far too much at freaking *work*...

My knees tremble.

My nighttime fantasies have been off the charts the last couple of nights.

Thankfully, Jackson isn't here and I don't need to be distracted by those fantasies, by the dreams, by the insatiable need that has me charging my vibrator every night.

I walk over to the table, sink into an empty seat between Smitty and the wall, feeling something settle in me when he bumps his shoulder against mine. "Where's Kailey and the rest of the crew?"

He smiles. "The girls took the twins to that new kids' movie." One big shoulder lifts then drops. "They said no hockey players allowed."

"No," Walker says, mouth curving. "They said no *loud* hockey players allowed"—he winks at me—"as in no loud hockey players who like to talk during previews and all the intense parts because they're nervous a movie for kids won't have a happy ending."

"Hey now," Smitty protests. "That shit gets intense some-times. Especially when they kill off Bambi's mom or whatever."

My gaze connects with Walker's across the table, and he rolls his eyes, but his mouth—just like mine—is curved up at the edges. "Dommie wants you to taste test a new cake flavor the bakery is trying out. You down?"

"This"—I wave a hand at my jaw—"sweet tooth is always

down for any consumption of baked goods, but especially those delicious baked goods loaded with sugar and covered in frosting your woman makes."

He grins. "I'll tell her to text you."

I nod, open my mouth to thank him, but the words don't make it past my lips.

Because my gaze slides over his shoulder at the sight of someone coming close—

No. Not *someone*.

Jackson is walking across the room, all loose-limbed grace and leanly muscled strength.

Our eyes connect, and I'm lost in the deep brown depths, breath trapped in my lungs, heart suddenly in my throat. Like amber stones glinting in the sunshine, so many shades of brown and gold and—

He blinks, and the connection breaks as he looks away, a muscle in his cheek flickering.

Heat crawls up my cheeks at his obvious dismissal.

"You good?" Smitty asks.

A shrug before Jackson hesitates to take the only empty seat at the table…

The one next to me.

His mouth flattens out, and I get a flash of that dog-poop-on-the-bottom-of-his-boot feeling before I shove that down and lift a brow in his direction.

A flicker of connection, of him responding to my nonverbal challenge.

Then he's glancing away again, dropping with a sigh into the seat next to me.

"I'm fine," Jackson mutters when Smitty shifts, as though getting ready to ask again, and adds, "I had to change my pump, something I've done a fuck-ton of times in my life. It's not rocket-science."

My gaze goes to between the men, wondering what Smitty's reaction is going to be to that obvious dismissal.

But there isn't one—or not *much* of one, anyway. Smitty just shrugs, lifts the pitcher in question to Jackson and then to me. Jackson nods. I shake my head.

"She doesn't like beer, dumbass," Jackson mutters.

Which makes Smitty's mouth quirk as he fills one chilled glass and slides it over to Jackson.

I don't get a chance to comment on the fact that Jackson knows I don't like beer because suddenly he's shoving his chair back and stalking across the room, moving with purpose to the bar and speaking with the bartender.

A few moments later, the man starts moving, mixing up a drink.

My heart tries to leapfrog out of my throat, especially when I see the glint of a copper mug, know that it's for a Moscow mule.

My drink of choice.

"Hmm," Smitty says quietly.

"What?"

But he doesn't answer, just turns to answer something that Raph asks him, and meanwhile, I'm watching Jackson pay for my drink and tip the bartender and...

Carry the drink back to the table.

Watching him set it gently in front of me.

I glance from the copper mug up to him. "Thanks," I say, almost expecting him to return to jerk, to spill it in my lap or something so I have to go home.

He doesn't.

He just sits in silence next to me.

And I sit in silence next to him.

And...I drink my drink.

And...he drinks *his* drink.

But I can't help but think that this is going to fuel my night-time fantasies as well.

An hour later, I'm ready for one more drink before I head home.

Normally, I would have left already, gone back to my bed and my blankets and my laptop filled with work, but Jackson slipped out a bit ago and the tension between my shoulder blades relaxed.

And Smitty has been telling a funny story filled with on-ice antics and…

Well, part of me doesn't want to go home yet.

Quietly, I push my chair back—

But quietly doesn't matter with these guys—they all turn to me.

"You heading home?" Smitty asks, big palms on the table, as though he's going to push himself up. "I'll walk you to your car."

I shake my head. "I'm just going to get one more drink before I head out."

"I can—"

I touch his shoulder, staying him. "I've got it. *Really,*" I tell Raph, Walker, and Cas when they open their mouths, the protests already forming on their faces. "I need to stretch my legs."

And then I get up and head to the bar.

Because that's the only way to handle these guys—stand firm on the battles I need to win and strategically retreat before they can work up any further protests.

Tonight, the battle I need to win is me buying my own drinks.

It's bad enough that Jackson got the first one.

I—

Need to stop thinking about him.

I wait for the bartender to notice me then order my drink.

He smiles, starts mixing, and I lean against the worn wood, my mind drifting to work.

There's the new social media coordinator to help train, several meetings with Luc about team maintenance—marketing, press, contracts, and the like, and—

"Hey."

For a second, I think it's the bartender and start to thank him, but then I realize as I've been thinking about work, a man's come close.

A very attractive man with a nice smile, striking blue eyes and medium blond hair. He's in shape and several inches taller than me. And he smells nice.

Too bad my body goes...*meh*.

Because I'm too focused on the fact that my nerves are on fire from having sat next to Jackson all night, our thighs occasionally brushing, his spicy scent in my nose—

Jesus. Just stop, Claire.

I want a family.

I want someone who'll like me for me, not play jerk because he's too scared to let anyone in and—

The man next to me flicks his brows up, and I realize I've been staring at him for far too long.

"H-hey," I stammer back.

He sticks out his hand. "I'm Matt."

My cheeks feel like they're on fire as I shake it. "H-hi, Matt."

His smile widens, his brows flick up again, warm fingers wrapping around mine. "What's your name, baby?"

That feels...

Strange. *Wrong*.

But I still say, "Claire. I'm Claire Jones." I shrug. "Pretty much the most boring name in history."

He chuckles...

And, heaven help me, but Operation Word Vomit commences.

"I actually come from a long line of Joneses, or am adopted into that line, anyway. But Joneses—that's plural for Jones and without the dreaded apostrophe or worse, the apostrophe and the extra s that people seem to default to on addresses. J-O-N-E-S-E-S. Anyway, my grandmother is a stickler for grammar and punctuation, so I try to make sure I don't cause her extra undue pain, you know? Because grandmothers are the coolest women around—or at least mine is. She knows how to properly use skibidi Ohio rizz like all the young kids and I swear, even they don't know what it means, and then she can go and make some of the best chocolate chip cookies you've ever tasted. She's super fun to hang with. Mostly because she adopted me and because we like to solve word puzzles while chowing down on ice cream together. Talk about the best kind of night, especially when there's bingo—"

"You know what?" Matt says, slipping his hand from mine and holding up his phone. "This is actually work. I have to take this call."

I only have a second to frown at the blank screen, indicating no incoming call, before he's gone, walking away and hurrying out of the room.

"That'll be twelve dollars."

"Here."

It's a familiar voice, same as the familiar hand that reaches forward and passes the bartender a twenty. "Keep the change." Then Smitty pushes the mule into my hands and orders, quietly—thank God, he somehow mastered how to be quiet for a few minutes, "Drink that. Christ. I'm dying of secondhand embarrassment over here."

My cheeks flare and I wince before I guzzle down some vodka. "I suck at dating."

"And talking apparently," he says lightly.

"Smitty," I groan, dropping my chin to my chest. "Really?"

He tugs a lock of my hair, tone still gentle. "It happens to the best of us."

"Does it?" I ask dryly. "Does it really?"

A wince. "Okay, so maybe not."

"Exactly." I sigh, torn between buying another drink so I can start double-fisting or running the hell out of this bar.

"Claire Bear?"

I look up at the suddenly gentle question—not a hint of teasing in sight.

"Yeah?"

Smitty tucks me against his big, warm side. "Don't worry. I've got a plan."

CHAPTER EIGHT

Jackson

"Be careful, honey bun."

"I'll be fine, Mom," I say, rolling my eyes at the worry in her tone. "It's hockey. It's a contact sport."

"I don't like seeing you get checked." A beat. "Or slashed. Or into fights that make you bleed."

"We know."

I grin when my dad chimes in over the speaker phone, his voice hard to hear because of the sound of running water in the background. It's just after lunch time back home and I know he's washing dishes.

My mom cooks. My dad does dishes. That's the way it's always been.

"But even your baby boy has to grow up some time," my dad finishes.

"Never," my mom protests. "And he doesn't have to do it getting beat to hell and back."

I shake my head, stifle a sigh at the familiar argument.

"You know he loves it," my dad says.

My mom sighs.

Because she knows she's lost. Because my dad is right.

I love playing hockey. It's not just my job—it's my heart and soul.

"Ugh," she grumbles, but I don't miss the sound of the water growing louder, know that she's walking across their kitchen with the familiar blue cabinets, leaning close and rising on tiptoe to kiss my dad on his cheek. "I hate it when you're right."

"I don't," my dad says cheerfully.

I grin as I turn into the parking lot. "I need to go," I tell them. "I'm at the rink."

Another sigh. "We'll be watching," she says on a mock grumble.

They always do—no matter the hour. "I love you guys."

"Love you, bud."

"Love you, honey bunny."

Smiling, I roll my eyes, and we exchange goodbyes as I pull into a parking spot, idling there until we hang up. And then my engine's off and I'm heading into the rink, brows yanking together when I see Smitty and Claire in deep conservation in the hall that leads to the public-facing dressing room.

The bulk of the staff isn't allowed in the actual locker room —where we shower and change. This arrangement gives us privacy, while PG-13 space is available for press and coaching staff and our equipment guys to have access to us.

And Claire.

Who's standing very close to Smitty.

Who's fucking married.

I start forward, strain to hear her words.

"I don't know if I can do that, Smitty. I—" She sighs. "I'm not good with that kind of thing and—"

"Sometimes you have to trust the process," he says, quietly for him but still easily discernible where I struggled to hear her. "Baby steps until you get comfortable. Eventually, you'll be at the finish line and will be able to look back and see that you did it."

That's good advice.

But if I was on the receiving end, I'd have the same reaction that Claire does.

Which is muttering begrudgingly, "Look back and see I struggled through something that's ridiculously easy for other people?"

"What's that saying?" Smitty asks. "Comparison is the thief of joy?"

Her nose wrinkles, and fuck that's cute. So cute I want to close the distance between us and bend down and kiss the bridge, want to—

Her eyes slide to the side, and I know the exact moment that she spots me.

Her shoulders tense up, her expression blanks out, and—

It's like when I sat next to her at CeCe's the other day.

She's only a few feet away—or in that case, mere inches—but she may as well be standing on the opposite side of a concrete wall, she's so untouchable. Something I need to remember. Something I fucking *have* to remember.

"Excuse me," I mutter gruffly, shoving by Smitty.

"Hot to trot?" he grumbles, rubbing the shoulder I bumped into.

"One of us has to be."

He just rolls his eyes and turns back to Claire. "I should get dressed," I hear him say. "But I'll talk to Kailey and see if she has any other ideas, yeah? But in the meantime, just try what I suggested?"

I'm turning to enter the locker room, that's the only reason I glance down the hall—my head's halfway there as it is. Or maybe…it's that I can't stop it, same as I can't stop the sliver of jealousy from sliding through me, the urge to rush toward Smitty and shove him until he's away from Claire, until he's not touching her, not close enough to scent her, not close enough to—

Claire nods and smiles up at him, then he opens his arms and she leans in, hugs him tightly.

The bolt of pain shooting through my jaw snaps me back to focus.

Enough.

Just...fucking *enough.*

I force my teeth apart, relieve the strain on my jaw, and tear my gaze away. There's fucking nothing to be jealous of. Smitty's just clearly being his normal meddling, annoying self, and—

I'm not jealous.

I'm fucking *not.*

And even as I try to convince myself of that fact, even as I know that I'm a fucking idiot playing with fire, it still takes everything in me to not stalk out of the room and back down the hall, to not rip her out of Smitty's arms, to not demand she tell me what in the fuck all she's in cahoots with my teammate about. As much as I try to tell myself it doesn't matter, it's not about me, that more distance is better, that it makes things less complicated, makes it easier for me to just do my fucking job...

I don't fucking believe it.

I want her to obsession. I need—

My watch buzzes on my wrist and I glance down.

My fucking pancreas to stop being an asshole.

But at least it pivots me from the hot mess in my mind.

I move to the bench, plunk down, and take care of the high notification—not a surprise since it's not just food that affects my numbers. Emotions and hormones and exercise, lack of sleep and too much stress (like trying to ignore the draw I have toward Claire) can fuck with keeping my glucose in range. Hell, half the time, I would swear that the lunar cycle affects how much insulin I need.

But that's life with diabetes.

It's rolling with the punches, adjusting to changes on the fly, and functioning on interrupted sleep.

It's also easier to deal with than the bullshit swirling in my head about Claire, about my past, about why I have to stay the fuck away from her.

I inhale, shove those memories down.

And then I focus on my own shit.

Not Smitty walking into the locker room, smirk in place, knowing glint in his eyes.

Not Claire bringing snacks and leaving my sandwich on the table instead of handing it to me like she normally does.

Not the Sierra, now the second most annoying team in the league to play against.

Not even the crowd, which goes crazy when I score three fucking goals and then blow off some steam when the Sierra try to claw their way back by fighting Lake Jordan. The bastard is far too pretty and smug for his own good, and though I can't call the on-ice fist exchange in my favor, I, at least, wiped the smirk off his face and got in a few good blows before I sat my ass in the box.

We win handily—which is a fucking feat against the Sierra on a normal night and something I would normally be celebrating.

But tonight, my gaze connects with Claire's the moment I push into the locker room.

And I'm right back to that night years before.

Right back in that nightmare.

Right back where I was when I realized that Claire knew the secret that can end my career.

Right back to when…

I realized exactly what kind of monster I am.

CHAPTER NINE

Claire

Smitty is a giant bully who makes people do things they don't want to.

Or I'm a pushover who's doing something I don't want to do.

Or...

Some combination of both those things is likely.

My cell dings and I straighten from the bar, pulse speeding through my veins, making me feel more than a little lightheaded.

Maybe he's not coming.

Maybe he *is*.

Maybe—

I turn over my cell and glance at the screen.

Not a message from the dating app Smitty convinced me to sign up for.

But a message from Smitty himself.

> You got this, kid! Remember, practice means perfect.

God, he's such a good guy. And a good friend. I smile and start to turn my cell over, intending to go back to my mule and watching the front door closely while trying to pretend I'm not doing exactly that when it buzzes again.

> Plus, if you fuck it up, we'll be in a new city tomorrow, so you never have to see the asshole who doesn't realize he's standing in the presence of perfection again.

That's both…

Sweet and a little rude.

Kind of like Smitty himself.

Shaking my head, my mouth kicking up further, I type out a response and hit the arrow to send it off.

Then it's back to waiting and sipping my mule and thinking about Smitty's pep talks and advice and—

Too antsy to sit still any longer, I give in and unlock my phone's screen, navigating to the notes app and scan through the shared file that Smitty and Kailey put together for my hopeless-at-small-talk self.

1. Do not go off on a tangent about apostrophes and unnecessary letters.

"Yeah," I mutter. "I definitely should have kept that tidbit to myself."

I almost don't blame the guy for running off.

Sighing, I look to the next item on the list.

2. Don't make yourself small just because you want some asshole to like you. You're perfectly special as you are.

Grimacing at Kailey's obvious addition to Smitty's tip, I move on down.

> 3. *Small talk is challenging, but there's always*
> *movies and hockey and funny TikToks to talk about.*
> *Don't be afraid to use these:*

And as my eyes look through the list of conversational topics and links to videos that Kailey provided below that advice—a tiny small-talk-defeating handbook of sorts—my belly warms. I may not be close to finding a partner, a happy-ending, a man who loves me for me and with all of my strange quirks, but at least I have Gran and Junie, and Smitty and Kailey, and the rest of the guys.

Jackson's face flashes across my brain, but I push it down.

I'm here for a date, here to have a good night, and I'm not going to worry about anyone else.

Not the man who hates me—or maybe doesn't.

Not—

I see a flash of movement in the mirrors behind the bar and watch as the door to the front of the restaurant opens, as a man comes through. Not the one tap-dancing through my mind, not the one who...I don't know, hates me, tolerates me, knows my favorite type of cocktail, touches me gently and says I'm a good person...

But the one from the dating app that Smitty convinced me to sign up for.

He's tall, taller than I expected and slender. Not the built solidness of Smitty, nor the muscled leanness of Jackson. But he's in good shape—I can tell that much even from this distance. It's the way he fills out the button down shirt and jeans, the confident stride as he approaches the hostess stand, as I watch him in the mirror have a short conversation before she turns to point in my direction.

I watch him in the reflection as his gaze traces over my body. I'm perched on the bar stool but I'm wearing a nice dress, the nicest little black dress I own, and I spent a long time curling my hair so it flows nicely down my back. I shift and start to turn—

When I see him look back at the hostess.

And smile.

And stay there and chat with her.

And pull out his phone, type something into it, and—

Smile at her again before…

He turns and walks out of the restaurant.

My whole body is still as I wait for the door to open again, for him to come back in, for the hostess to come over and give me some sort of explanation—he forgot to buy me flowers or a puppy or—

My cell chimes and I lurch for it, seeing a message push notification pop up on the screen from the dating app. I click into it, heart in my throat as I wait for it to load.

Sorry, I have to cancel. I got stuck at work.

I'm frozen for a few seconds, staring at the words, wondering if I could have imagined the man walking in, imagined the whole interaction with the hostess at the front of the bar.

But his…picture is right there.

It was him.

He saw me…

And he got the fuck out.

I—

My skin is too tight for my body and my eyes burn like motherfuckers, but I manage to sit there and finish my drink, manage to pay and tip the bartender—and do it seeming sort of normal, I think.

Or at least, he doesn't give me any strange looks.

Then I'm out of the bar, out onto the sidewalk.

And clearly, out of my mind thinking that any man might want me.

———

Turns out that chasing down the perfect gas station hot dog after spending the night tossing and turning, mind on repeat as I relived the scene in the bar, the look I'd seen my supposed date giving me in the mirror, the flirting with the hostess, the confident swagger as he made his way out...

Well, none of that is conducive to sleep.

I inhale, shore up my spine, and hold my sack of snacks closer, grip the cooler full of drinks I'm wheeling behind me tighter.

I'll sleep tonight—exhaustion will make that so, I think, considering how damned tired I am already and the game hasn't even started yet.

We've got more games to go too.

More cities to see.

More dates—

To cancel because I'm not doing that shit again.

I inhale, push through the door, trying to keep my eyes on target—the table on the far side of the room where I can set up my stuff.

Unfortunately, my gaze drifts up, hitches when it meets Jackson's for the barest of a second.

Scalding.

Judging.

Yeah, no. I don't need any more of that.

Not after yesterday. Not after—

"Something caught your eye, Jackson?"

I jump and hurry to the table, ignoring Smitty's arch question, ignoring Jackson's sharp retort, ignoring the other chatter and teasing as I hurriedly set up the guys' pregame snacks.

"Thanks for the drinks, Clairey girl!" Smitty calls, as I turn around, his voice ringing around the room.

My cheeks flash fiery hot, and I fight the urge to bolt, wanting nothing of his piercing brown eyes that see far too much, his dog-with-a-bone mentality to ferret out gossip.

Wanting nothing to do with Jackson and all the complicated feelings he has churning in my stomach.

My shoulders hunch, but I force them to relax as I lift my head, plaster on a smile, and nod. "You're welcome," I tell him. "Let me know if you need anything else."

I start for the door.

"How was your date?"

Dammit.

I pick up my pace, definitely going for avoidance now, but even though I'm not looking at Smitty, I feel my cheeks burn hotter.

Can I make it into the hall without raising suspicion?

A quick flick of my eyes to his tells me enough.

Nope. I sure can't.

"It was fine, Smitty," I say, hoping he'll listen to the unspoken note in my tone and leave it the hell alone.

Smitty, though, doesn't leave it alone.

"*Fine* doesn't exactly scream a good date," he says, loudly as always.

I grind my teeth together, go straight avoidance even though I know he'll press me for answers later. "Bye, Smitty."

"Did he do something?"

I freeze.

Because that didn't come from Smitty.

I slowly spin to face Jackson, whose tone is steely and expression is hard as granite.

"Did he hurt you?" he asks, not in Smitty-volume, but

loudly enough to be heard throughout the entire room, and everyone falls quiet, sending their focus to me.

"It's not like that," I hedge, moving to the door even more quickly. Escape. I need to escape because I cannot have this conversation. "I have other things—"

Jackson is suddenly in front of me, strong, warm fingers wrapping around my arm. "Did. He. Hurt. You?" he growls.

This from the man who's done his level best to push me away?

Who left me thinking he hates me more often than not?

Who—

Fucking hell.

I don't want to do this.

Not here. Not now. Not *ever*.

I lift my chin and glare at him, yanking my arm free and shoving at his chest.

Of course, he doesn't fucking move.

Ugh. Hockey players.

Especially when he reaches for me again.

"Don't you fucking touch me," I snap, oddly pleased when he drops his hand back to his side, even as the edge of my temper doesn't ease. "He stood me up, okay?" I take a step back, anger and embarrassment propelling me toward the door. "Only he didn't." I toss up my hands and blurt out the rest of the awful truth. "Not really, anyway. Because I watched in the mirror behind the bar as he walked through the restaurant door, took one look at me—"

Jackson's face blanches.

"—and turned right around again and strolled on out."

CHAPTER TEN

Jackson

"So, YEAH, HE HURT ME," Claire says, her voice laced with pain. "Just not how you think."

The locker room goes quiet, awkward, and I feel like a dick, having pushed Claire to answer the question in the first place.

I just...

It never fucking crossed my mind to think that someone would stand her up—or that, worse, someone would get a look at her and not want to worship at her fucking feet.

Beautiful, sweet, quiet, but with a spine of steel, Claire deserves the world.

It's why I've fought what I'm feeling, fought the urge to keep my distance, did my fucking level best to make sure I didn't get close enough to let my bullshit hurt her.

And that fucker who was supposed to take her on a date had hurt her.

So...I'm going to kill the bastard.

She spins on her heel before I can get his full name, address, and social security number, and hurries from the room.

And...I don't think.

I just follow her, trailing her until we're out of earshot, letting her put some space between us and the locker room. But I catch her arm when she turns the corner and would've stepped into a hall with a floor that isn't covered with skate mats.

A hall that has a floor where I can't follow her.

"Claire," I say, drawing her back against me.

And it's like every ragged edge in my soul is suddenly smoothed over—sharp, broken edges are softened, sanded down, left unblemished and unmarked.

"Don't," she whispers.

I can't.

Yet, I can't stop myself.

I spin her so she's facing me, cup her cheek in one palm, willing her to understand how fucking precious she is. "He's an asshole and you deserve better."

Her eyes flick to mine, and then away, and the pain in the deep brown depths calls to me, spurs me on. I have to make her understand that, have to make sure she knows how fucking great she is. "Sure," she says quietly, the four letters filled with disbelief.

Rage fills my belly, burns up the back of my throat.

How does this woman not see how fucking perfect she is?

And...fuck it.

I'm going to make her see.

I have to.

"Claire," I begin.

"I'm fine," she whispers, trying to pull free.

But I'm done with this, done with keeping my distance. I draw her with me as I turn and move us through a door and into one of the empty rooms lining the hallway, closing it behind us, pinning her back against the wooden panel.

She's tall for a woman, but I'm taller, especially in my skates. "You're not fine."

Her chin lifts. "I am fine."

"Liar."

She shoves at my chest and when that doesn't move me, she tosses her hands up. "It wasn't going to work long-term anyway, I knew that going in."

"Why wouldn't it work?"

She frowns at me. "Um...because I live in Baltimore and can't have a states away boyfriend?"

Snark.

Sass.

This woman only gives them to me.

And I fucking love it.

"So, why did you go on the date in the first place?" My hands are on either side of her head and I sneak them in a little, allowing my fingertips to brush the silken ends of her ponytail.

So fucking soft.

Like I know the rest of her will be.

Her cheeks go pink. "It doesn't matter."

And that reaction tells me that it matters a whole fucking lot. "Claire," I warn.

She scowls at me. "Don't pull that big, broody hockey player nonsense. You can't bully me into giving you an answer and—"

"—you don't owe me any explanation of your life," I finish, am able to because she's told us guys on the team the same thing enough times that I've memorized her answer.

Those eyes narrow further. "Exactly."

"So," I say, ignoring the laser beams she's tossing my direction and pushing for an answer anyway. "Did you just need to get laid?"

Pink turns to bright red, and she shoves harder at my chest. "You're an asshole, you know that, right?"

"Yup."

It's why I've waited so long to be here.

To touch her.

To feel the lush curves of her body pressed to mine.

A huffed-out breath. "Back up," she snaps. "I have work to do."

"Been a long time, kitty cat?" I ask, leaning more heavily against her, wishing I wasn't mostly dressed in my gear, wishing I could feel her naked skin against my own.

"I—no."

But there's something in her tone, in the way panic enters her eyes that has me freezing, leaning even closer, studying her face.

"Why then?"

Her jaw clenches and I know she's not going to tell me—know that I can push and push, but that she'll double down and won't fucking *tell* me.

I inhale the sweet scent of her, commit the notes of it to memory.

And then I avoid pushing and commence with...pissing her off.

That'll get her to talk.

Hell, it may be the only way right about now.

"So," I say dryly, "you're getting enough dick at home that you don't need sex. What then?" I tap a finger to my chin, watching as her frown deepens. "You just want a guy to buy you dinner and drinks?"

She sputters. "That's n-not—"

"Ah, I see. Don't worry. I'm sure I can talk to someone and put in a good word for you with Luc," I cajole. "See about getting you a raise. Or maybe I'll talk to the guys and do a collection, get you some gift cards for Red Lobster or something."

Her eyes say she's going to kill me.

But the devil in me can't stop.

Not when I need to her tell me, even if she does it while being pissed.

"Not Red Lobster?" I say. "Fine." I sigh. "You drive a hard bargain, but I'm sure I can swing a meal at The Cheesecake Factory—"

"Fuck. *You*," she hisses.

I shrug and then push a button I know will get her talking. "It's not me who's trying to get laid while on the road."

"I told you—" she growls and shoves at my chest. "I didn't want sex or a free meal. I just wanted to go on a real date—" She clamps her lips together, cheeks flaring, eyes darting away, chin dropping.

Fuck.

A *real* date?

"Sweetheart," I rumble.

Her head flies up. "Don't," she snaps, jabbing a finger into my chest. "Don't pretend to care about me."

"That's not fair, I—"

I want to say I do care, but that would involve admitting shit that I can't and…

Fuck.

"Let me go."

"No," I growl, stepping closer, trapping her hand between us.

Maybe I can't tell her everything, but I can make this better, can solve this problem—

And then what?

I walk away.

Yes.

God, I don't fucking want to.

I don't even think I can.

Not if I allow myself—

But the emotional shitstorm in my mind doesn't matter.

Because she's rolling her eyes and snapping, "Okay fine. You want to know my sad sob story? *Really?* You do, right? You want to know the whole pathetic truth? I've never been laid, okay?"

Every muscle in my body tightens.

"I've never even been on a real date. Hell, I'm so pathetic" —she tosses up her hands again—"that I've never even been kissed!"

She's fucking beautiful.

And furious and smart and sweet and untouched, apparently, and—

I give in.

Mine.

The most important thing is that she's mine.

I cup her jaw again, tilt her face up. "Well, I can at least solve that one for you."

Her brows draw together. "What—?"

No more words.

We've exchanged enough fucking words these last seasons.

It's time for action.

So, I bend…

And press my mouth to hers.

CHAPTER ELEVEN

Claire

I'm frozen.

Locked in place.

Pinned between a hard body and a hard door and…

Jackson Hunter is kissing me.

Me.

His fingers flex on my cheek and I look up into deep chocolate pools as he ends the kiss. He doesn't move away, though, leaves our mouths close enough that our lips brush with every breath.

"Your eyes are like Willy Wonka," I blurt.

Confusion then amusement in those pools I want to jump into and devour, drink and drink and *drink* until I can't take in any more.

His thumb brushes beneath my bottom lashes but he doesn't back up, just speaks as I had, our mouths tangling with each new word formed. "*Your* eyes are like dark chocolate. I want to spread it on your naked body and lick it off inch by luscious inch."

I shiver, blurt again, "You kissed me."

"I did." He bends a little. "You didn't kiss me back."

I hadn't, I realize. I just stood here, pressed to the door by all of his lean strength, and...didn't do anything except spew weird awkwardness about fucking Willy Wonka.

My cheeks burn, and I know they've got to be bright red, but before I can say something—*anything*—to make this whole thing less cringey and intense, Jackson keeps talking.

"Is it because I overstepped?" he asks softly. "Or because you don't know how?"

My lungs inflate in a rapid rush that has me choking on my own spit. "I—" I cough, bending at the middle, nearly braining myself on his hard shoulder. "I—"

"Easy," he murmurs softly, returning his hand to my cheek, slipping his other behind me and settling it between my shoulder blades, drawing me against his body. He smooths his palm slowly up and down my back. "Easy now, kitty cat."

I'm dying of embarrassment inside.

But his touch, the soft words and steady stroking settle me in a way that I'm never felt before.

Like my body knows it can finally take a breath, can finally ease some of the heavy load off my shoulders.

Can just *be*.

And for a moment, I do just that—stand in the circle of his arms, inhaling the scent of him, feeling the strength of him.

Then...

I remember myself.

What I admitted. What I'm doing *now*.

I jerk back so fast that I whack my head against the door.

"Ow," I groan, rubbing the aching spot—

At least until my hand is brushed away. "I told you easy, sweetheart," he chastises quietly, gently massaging the spot. "You're going to hurt yourself."

"You told me a lot of things," I mutter. "But I—"

"I'm an asshole," he says baldly. "And I was fucking scared when you found what you found—"

"I—"

"You wouldn't use it against me." Gentle fingers sifting through my hair. "I know that now. I just...I'm not a good person, kitty cat."

I think he's wrong.

I know it. Just like I know he's a good person—yeah, he's cranky and tries to keep people at a distance and technically did something really bad, but he did it for the right reasons.

And I know something about keeping people at a distance.

I just...don't want to do that, not now, not here, not—

When I feel more alive in this stolen moment with Jackson than I ever had before.

"It wasn't too much," I tell him, turning the conversation away from what had made him so angry with me months ago, what had made me feel so freaking guilty for pursuing information that wasn't any of my business. I was nosy and I was protective of the team and...I was wrong. But I don't want to think about that, think about the circumstances that wrote that pain into the lines of his face, that left such a mark. I want him to...

Focus on me, I guess.

"I was surprised," I say, my cheeks flaring again, but I push on. "And I didn't think you liked me—and I guess..."

"What?" he asks gently.

Hide? Shrink into the embarrassment?

Or just...be honest and truthful and *myself*?

I already know the answer.

"I certainly didn't think you could like me like this."

A random stranger turned and bolted upon sight of me.

A hot bachelor hockey player with his choice of women?

Why would he pick me?

"And," I whisper. "I...don't know what I'm doing. I—

kissing and dating and—" My courage fails me, and I tear my gaze from his.

He's silent for a long moment, but when he does speak, his words take my breath away. "So…we practice."

I gulp. "Wh-what?"

His smile…good God, it makes my knees weak. "We practice, kitty cat." He leans in, brushes his lips over my forehead. The tip of my nose. Each cheek. "We practice until you're confident." A kiss to the hinge of my jaw. "We practice until you don't want to practice anymore."

"Pr-practice k-kissing?" I sputter. "W-with y-you?"

His smile is…

Well, it's something I know that will revisit me in my dreams.

Maybe that's why I blurt again, "I know how to make myself come."

His brows shoot up to his hairline, but his smile doesn't fade. Instead, it transforms…

Into something wicked.

"You do, kitty cat?" He drops his head until our lips are almost aligned again, until I can feel the damp heat of his words against my mouth. "You'll show me how you do that."

Not a question.

A statement.

And…I shiver. Because I know that if he asks me to show him, I will.

Something I know *he* recognizes because that wicked smile stays in place as he says, "Good, kitty cat. Now, stop over-thinking it and just follow my lead."

I open my mouth to ask *what lead?* but I don't get the chance.

Because then his lips are on mine again.

The shock of sensation is real and intense and makes my knees shaky. Jackson is kissing me. Jackson. Is kissing. *Me*. It's too much to process and that's not even bringing into account what I should be doing with my hands or my body or—

God.

My lips.

I'm supposed to be doing stuff with my lips, with my tongue. All the really hot kissing in movies and in books involves tongue—

Jackson lifts his head. "Kitty cat."

I blink. "Y-yeah?"

"Close your eyes."

God, I'm supposed to be doing stuff with my eyes too—namely not leaving them wide open as I stare at him incomprehensibly.

"Claire."

I swallow hard, search for an escape. Because, fuck, this is too embarrassing. What I've revealed, what I've done. It's too fucking much. I need the floor to open and swallow me up...or to find another way the hell out of this room. Thankfully, the fact that he's wearing his hockey gear—most of it, anyway—gives me that escape.

"You need to get ready for the game." I lift my head, check the time on my watch, feel my heart skip a beat or twenty. "It's fifty minutes before game time," I squeak. "You need your sandwich and—"

His hand settles on my jaw again, and he tilts my head up, forcing my gaze back to his.

He doesn't say anything, just studies me for a long moment.

Then he leans in again and even as I start to worry about what the hell I should be doing with my eyes, my hands, my body and lips and tongue, he bypasses my mouth.

Up. Up.

Above my lips. By my nose. Skipping my cheeks.

And...

Leans close, so close that my eyes close by instinct.

He presses a kiss to each lid.

I exhale, feel my body start to soften.

And then he's running his hand up my side, making me shiver, making me melt against him. His mouth drags down my cheek, along my jaw, back behind my ear. "Shh, sweetheart," he murmurs when a flick of his tongue has me squeaking and jumping against him. That sleek dart of damp heat comes again, and though I still jump, I relax faster, my hands settling on his chest without thinking, my nails digging in when he sucks lightly on sensitive spot near the hinge of my jaw.

He grunts.

"Oh," I say, my eyes flying open, realizing I'm scratching him, that I'm hurting him. *Shit.* I start to pull back.

He clamps a hand over mine. "Don't," he orders softly. "I like it."

"I—"

He nips at my bottom lip, making me squeak again. "Close your eyes."

I should protest the command, should stop this.

But instead, I just keep my hands where they are and...I allow my lids to drift closed.

His lips press to each of them in turn again, and then he kisses the bridge of my nose, the corner of my mouth, my bottom lip.

I exhale sharply.

"That's it," he murmurs. "Keep it open for me."

And then his mouth is settling over mine, gently, slowly, our lips fused together, soft and open and—

He slips his tongue through the gap and brushes it along mine.

I gasp, lips parting further, which seems to be exactly what he wants because he makes a sound of approval, leans more heavily against me, and strokes his tongue a little more firmly, a little deeper, a little—

My moan slips up my throat, dances across my tongue, and...

Something incredible happens.

He groans, the sound vibrating through me, sending shock waves of pleasure through my breasts, my belly, arrowing down between my thighs. That's great—feels fucking great—but it's not the wonderful part. Nope. *That* happens when he kisses me more deeply...

And when I stop thinking so hard about it.

My lips move without my direction, matching his rhythm, my tongue coming out to tangle with his.

The kiss...

Is incredible.

My body reacts like it's meant to kiss this man, like I was put on this planet to be in this room, to feel him, to touch him, to experience this stolen moment with him.

Jackson pulls back, his eyes hot, his lips a little swollen. "Fucking perfect," he murmurs, resting his forehead against mine.

My nerves are on fire. My head is spinning. I'm half-convinced if he lets me go that I'll collapse into a puddle of goo.

The only thing that makes me feel better is that Jackson is as out of breath as I am.

"You good?" he asks.

Good? I feel like I'm floating...or that I need to go back to the hotel room and get my vibrator so I can ease this ache between my legs.

"You're good," he says, mouth curving, thumb brushing along my jaw, pressing down lightly on my bottom lip so he can lean in to taste me again.

And this time, I don't feel awkward or embarrassed. I'm not worried about my hands or eyes. I just...

Kiss Jackson Hunter.

Until my head feels like it's spinning.

Until I forget that it's almost forty-two minutes before game time.

Until—

Knock. Knock. *Knock!*

This pause in time and space, this secret moment...

Is broken.

"Fuck," he mutters, pulling back and resting his forehead against mine. "We need to go."

"Yes."

But neither of us move for a long moment.

At least until I lift a hand to my mouth. "My lips are tingling."

He grins then sobers, eyes gentling. "Like I said...perfect."

My heart skips a beat.

"Do I need to come in there?" Smitty booms through the door.

Jackson groans, his head dropping back. But then he straightens and meets my eyes, his smile rueful now.

"I'll see you after the game?"

CHAPTER TWELVE

Jackson

I eat my sandwich late, but for once, it doesn't affect my game play.

Probably because I'm already fixated on lithe curves, floral-scented shampoo, and a woman who tastes of sweet innocence and dangerous temptation.

I shouldn't be the one to corrupt her.

But I'm going to do it anyway.

I *have* to.

It's less want than obsession and—

I'm not good. I'm done pretending to be, trying to be, desperate to be.

I'm going to take what I want and keep taking it until she sends me away.

I scoop up the puck, even though it's bouncing and not all that great of a pass, corralling it on the blade of my stick, and sprinting up the ice. I'm skating harder, moving faster and with more confidence than normal.

And I know it's because Claire is watching.

Because the ego in me wants to impress her—*needs* to impress her.

I can still feel those curves against my front, still taste her on my tongue, still hear her soft moans in my ears.

A sharp slash across my hands focuses me. I lose the puck for a second and have to scramble to regain control as I sprint through the neutral zone and try to make my way into the net. It's not easy and I spend what feels like an eternity just holding on to the puck and looking for an option.

Drive to the net?

Thread a pass through the center.

Back to my point?

The corner and behind the net?

Nothing is great at the moment, so I dance around the other team, dish the puck to myself with a pass off the boards, and try to be patience and creative and…effective.

Effective ends up being bringing the puck to the boards, holding it there, waiting for Aiden to come bail me out.

Grunting, keeping my feet under me by pure dint, grinding my teeth together when I get a crosscheck to the back but not rising to the bait they're trying to create, I slap a lid on my temper, hold fast and—

"Boxie."

As in jack-in-the-box, as in the nickname the team has christened me with, as in—

Aiden sweeping in to help me.

I clock in his reflection in the glass and…

Kick the puck to the side.

My teammate's the shit. He's good. Great really. And that means he's ready for the puck, even though my kick pass is blind and not completely accurate.

He sweeps it up, makes a nice deke, and whips it back to Smitty, who's cutting hard to the net.

I lean against the fucker who was slamming his stick into my back, delaying him long enough to make it tough to get to

Smitty but not enough to get the interference penalty. Then I'm pushing off the boards, hustling my ass to the goal, creating chaos and trying to not get hit in the ass by Smitty's hard-as-fuck shot.

The *crack* of the stick.

The *crunch* of my skates on the ice.

The roar of the crowd.

He gets the shot off, and it whizzes uncomfortably close behind my unpadded back. Thank fuck, though, I'm out of the way and then I'm crashing the net, locking my stick with one of the fucker's on the other team, digging at the rebound that bounces out, trying to shove it in behind the goalie.

The whistle comes before I can get it that far.

Fuck.

There's pushing and shoving, curse words and crosschecks, and then the refs are in the scrum, pushing us apart, shoving us toward our respective benches—and making sure we go instead of drawing each other into fights that'll land us five minutes in the penalty box.

I drop down onto the metal plank next to Aiden and Walker, my other linemate, and we take a few seconds to catch our breath, drink some water, and then we're game-planning for our next shift, eyes glued to the game, watching for any breakdowns we can exploit or openings we can take advantage of.

And the game goes on.

Back and forth, shift by shift, grinding out each and every play until—fucking finally—we get a couple of goals.

And keep that lead all the way to the final buzzer.

I drop my bottle into the holder and push up from the bench, my legs heavy and tired as I fist bump my teammates and then head down the hallway for the locker room.

I'm almost there before I feel it.

Feel *her.*

Pulse stuttering, I glance over and see her coming down

the hall. She's changed into her usual game day outfit of jeans and a nice blouse, topped with a blazer that has the Breakers logo emblazoned above the breast pocket.

Fuck, she's beautiful.

I peel off from the line, nearly running Smitty over in the process. But I ignore my pain in the ass teammate, ignore what's no doubt going to be a smirk on his face, ignore that he'll likely give me shit for this later and get his gossip jollies on in the meantime.

I just close the distance between Claire and me.

Her throat works as I stop with barely a foot between us, not wanting to get my sweat all over her, cognizant of the fact that her flats are no protection against my skates.

But I do slip my hand from my glove, lift it, and gently tuck a strand of her hair behind her ear.

"Hey," I say inanely.

"Hey," she says back, cheeks going pink.

I open my mouth to ask for her room number, knowing that we're not relocating tonight because we'll be playing the other New York team the night after next, but I stop.

Because—

I just wanted to go on a real date...

I can talk my way into her room, maybe even into her pants, but—

A real date.

She deserves that and so much more, deserves the fucking world.

And that's not going to happen if I have her room number.

It can happen if I'm smart, if I take care of her, if I make sure to give her all she deserves before she wises up and kicks my ass to the curb.

"Meet me in the morning for breakfast?" I ask softly, mind already spinning. We're in New York City—if there's ever a place to give someone the world, it's here.

"Breakfast?" she whispers.

"Yeah," I whisper back, my mouth hitching up in the corners.

She blinks, a flurry of emotions cascading across her expression, too fast for me to tease out.

But then her chin is coming up, her shoulders are straightening, and she nods.

"I'll meet you in the lobby at ten."

CHAPTER THIRTEEN

Claire

I nibble at my bottom lip and hesitate just outside the sunlit lobby, gaze searching for Jackson, half expecting this to be some sort of cruel joke.

That Jackson will come to his senses and not show up.

That I'll be standing here feeling inadequate until I manage to make my legs work enough to go back to my room and hide.

"Coming through!"

I realize that I'm blocking the hallway leading from the elevators to the lobby itself and jump to the side, allowing the employee with a huge cart through.

Not that I have a choice—it's either that or find myself beneath the rattling wheels as he determinedly makes his way across the lobby.

It's not just the man who's making noise, the entire space is busy with activity. There are people checking out, the aforementioned staff zipping through, shoes clicking on the marble floor as they accomplish their various tasks for the day. Across the other side of the sunshine-dappled room, the restaurant, currently serving breakfast, is hopping—including a large conglomerate of the Breakers crew consuming all manner of waffles and pancakes, cereal and granola, fruit and coffee.

Yeah, it's ten in the morning.

But hockey is played late into the night—three hours for the game (unless it goes to overtime, in which case they end even later). Then there are press conferences and post-game cool downs and workouts. Add in meeting with the training staff to address an injury or to keep the guys feeling good enough to endure the brutal eighty-two game season and early mornings aren't the norm.

Not if we can help it, anyway.

We, because I work with Luc and the team in charge of travel plans to try to make it as easy on the guys and staff as possible.

"Kitty cat."

I jump again, but this time it's to whip around and slam into a big, strong chest.

Jackson's not as tall as yesterday since he's not wearing his skates, but the moment his body meets mine, I feel it.

It.

Why it hurt when I thought he hated me.

Why my stomach was in knots thinking that he might not show this morning, that he might change his mind and leave me standing here, alone and—

"Don't."

I blink.

"Don't think that."

"What are you talking about?" I whisper as his hand lifts and cups my chin, as he tilts my head and pins me in place with his deep brown gaze.

"No more thinking I hate you." A gentle sweep of his thumb over my bottom lip. "And no more lies," he murmurs. "I stayed away before because I know I'm not good for you."

I open my mouth to protest but he doesn't give me the chance to form words.

Lightly, he presses down on my lips. "No, sweetheart. You know why."

And I get it then—the insane reality this man is living in. I want to argue, to speak against those fingers on my lips, to make him see what I see. But...

I also don't want to ruin this moment.

I'm going on a date with Jackson Hunter, with the man I've wanted and fantasized about in equal measure.

It might all blow up in my face—hell, it likely *will* blow up in my face, there's no *might* about it.

But...I want this.

I need it.

I—

"I'm not good for you," he says again, more quietly, not bothering to hide the pain in his eyes, the shadows of the past. They call to mine, to those old and deep wounds that never seem to fully heal. "But I need to give you this," he murmurs, brushing his thumb over my cheek. "I need to give you today."

"Wh—"

Only, he's already bending, sealing his mouth over mine, kissing me right here in the lobby, like he doesn't care who sees me, like he doesn't care if the *team* sees us—

That thought ricochets through my head in an instant, and I snap back, pulling my lips from his. "The guys—"

"Don't give a fuck," he mutters, weaving his fingers into my hair, drawing me back to him, tasting me slow and deep and easy. So slow that I'm not scared or too frozen to match his pace. So deep that desire blooms in my belly, spreads out to my limbs. So easy that I'm not thinking about all the things I don't know how to do, all the things I'm not confident about, all the things I might do wrong.

I'm just here.

With him.

"I don't understand," I finally murmur, when he pulls back but doesn't release me.

His fingers sweep lightly over my temple. "Don't understand what, kitty cat?"

My heart feels like it's going to pound out of my chest and my legs might as well be jelly. But Jackson doesn't let me go, just holds me against him. "This is just...you're kissing me, holding me, and you hated me—"

"*No.*"

The word is fierce enough to snap me out of my pleasure-filled haze.

"I know," I say, shaking my head, smoothing my hand along his chest. "I mean. I understand now that it wasn't really hate." I take a breath. "But this is...a whirlwind, Jackson. I-I'm spinning here—one second you were scowling at me, the next you were chasing me down the halls, and then we were kissing—*are* kissing and going on a date—" I nibble at my bottom lip. I should just roll with this, not try to make it make sense, especially when, God knows, it *won't* make sense, and when I've had to roll with so many things in my life.

It's just...

Some part of me needs the explanation, needs the pieces to fit together perfectly, needs—

His face gentles.

Needs *that.*

Understanding. Gentleness. The soft brush of his hand along my jaw, his lips pressing to my forehead. "It's a lot to throw at you."

His words are less question than statement, but I nod anyway. "I feel like I'm spinning like one of those reflective lawn ornaments, around and around and around."

"Cute," he murmurs, trailing his fingers down my throat. "Always so fucking cute."

I frown. "Me spinning?"

A shake of his head. "The things you say. The way you look at me. Your soft moans on my tongue—"

I inhale.

His mouth hitches up. "The pink on your cheeks. The freckles on the bridge of your nose. The way you nibble at your bottom lip." He softly frees said lip with his thumb.

"Jackson," I say.

"Come on." He takes my hand, spinning me and tucking me against his side, draping his arm around my shoulders as he draws me through the lobby, by the group of Breakers' players and staff, who are all staring unabashedly, and toward the spinning door at the front of the hotel.

"Where are we going?" I whisper.

He pauses then grins down at me suddenly, his smile beyond sexy.

"The best first date of your life."

CHAPTER FOURTEEN

Jackson

I shepherd Claire through the lobby, ignoring that Smitty's watching me like I'm a ticking time bomb.

You'd think that the matchmaking, gossip-monger would love that I'm finally giving in to the urge to pursue Claire.

Instead...

I've got furrowed brows and glaring eyes.

Cool. Cool.

I glare right back, tuck her a little closer, and guide Claire through the plate glass door that the porter swings wide for us, skipping the spinning door in lieu of keeping her close.

"Thanks, Tony," I mutter, passing him a hundred. He saved my ass last night and this morning, helping me organize shit that I stayed up far too late putting together.

Claire hasn't had a first date.

I need to make today fucking spectacular. She deserves that much.

And...I haven't given in to the urge to spend time with her before now, so I'm going to soak in every fucking moment.

She pauses when we make it out to the sidewalk and glances up at me. "Which way are we heading?" she asks, her voice melodic, her cheeks pink, her lips slightly swollen.

Back up to my room so I can give her a completely different kind of kiss.

But...

Date. Not fucking.

Making this special, making it *perfect*. Not taking advantage.

I nod toward the limo idling at the curb. "There," I say, drawing her forward.

A glance at the limo. Then at me. Then back to the curb. "Where—?"

"In the car, kitty cat," I order softly, nodding my thanks at the driver when he pulls open the door.

"It's not a car. It's a limo."

Amusement in my belly. "In the *limo*, sweetheart."

Another glance at me before she folds herself in with an adorable grunt, her movements somehow both cute and klutzy mixed together, especially when she hits her head against the fabric-covered ceiling. "Ow," she whispers, rubbing her head.

I brush her hands away, gentle massage the spot. "Better?" I ask a few moments later.

"Yeah." A shrug. "I'm always doing that, always running into things. It's why I don't ever get on the ice even though Luc and Smitty have both tried to teach me."

My brows draw together. "I've seen you out there before."

At charity events and team bonding get togethers.

She scowls and that's fucking adorable too. "Only because Smitty forced me to. I'm not cut out for flying around out there on skinny metal blades, all while attempting to avoid plowing into other people and not kill myself in the process."

I grin, remembering then that she *had* ended up on that lush ass a time or dozen, and pull out the basket of baked goods I picked up for her—including a half-dozen chocolate muffins. There not Dommie's, but they'll have to do. "I could teach you," I offer, holding out the basket.

"Nope," she says, popping the p, and I don't miss that she snags one of those muffins. "You could *try* but it would be a failure because I'm hopeless. See these?" She lifts a jean-clad leg. The material is skintight and showing off curves I've admired far too often. "*These* are weak ankles. No matter how good the skate, I can't keep from looking like a baby deer out there."

"Bambi," I say, remembering the guys teasing her with the nickname.

Her nose wrinkles. "Yup. That's where Smitty's moniker came from." A beleaguered smile. "Though, thankfully, he seems to have forgotten it in lieu of Clairey Girl of late."

"He hasn't forgotten," I tease, taking my own muffin, prompting her to unpeel the wrapper of hers and start eating. "He's just biding his time, waiting for the precise right moment to bring it back out again."

A giggle. "You're probably right, *Boxie*."

"Hey," I shrug. "At least my nickname isn't Glitter."

Her eyes dance as she giggles again. "True."

Then we fall quiet as we finish our food, and I find myself at a loss for what to say. Bantering with her feels right, feels better than anything except for touching her, kissing her...

But it's not enough.

And yet, at the same time, I don't want to make this about the past, about my fuckups, about me not being a good person.

I want her to have a great fucking day.

Bar none. Hands down. Without question. Effortlessly—

I'm rambling.

In my own fucking mind.

Christ.

"What?" she asks.

"I think I get what that whirlwind is you're experiencing."

"Is it too much?" she asks. "We can go back—"

I reach across the empty space, take her hand. "I don't want to go back."

Her throat works. "I don't either," she whispers. "I like this." She nibbles at her bottom lip. "Just talking with you without all the..." She waves a hand.

Without all of *my* bullshit.

"I like talking to you too."

"Even though I'm a rambling virgin who's terrible at small talk?" Her lips curve at the corners, teasing all over that question. Except...

For the note of seriousness in her eyes.

"How did that happen anyway?"

I almost regret the question the moment it slips off the tip of my tongue and flits into the air between us. But I *need* to know.

"The usual way," she says lightly. "Only child to two deadbeats means I didn't have a ton of time to practice, and then by the time I trusted Gran enough to let her in, we mostly discussed ice cream, proper grammar, and game shows on TV."

I lightly squeeze her hand, knowing I should let her have that.

But I can't.

"I want to hear more about your parents," I say softly. "And Gran too, but I have to know, kitty cat, did someone hurt you and—"

"You're always worried about people hurting me," she says quietly.

Most of all worried about me hurting her.

But also...deadbeat parents and a troubled childhood.

"You deserve to feel safe," I remind her.

Another flicker across her eyes.

"What?"

"Gran used to say that all the time..." Her face softens.

"Used to say it so often that I'd scoff...until I eventually felt safe with her."

"You lived with her growing up?"

A shake of her head. "She's not actually my biological grandmother. She—" Her lips press flat and release. "I probably shouldn't be rambling about this on a first date."

"Maybe not," I admit, releasing her hand, but only so I can draw her closer, bring her body flush against mine, shoulder to shoulder, waist to waist, thigh to thigh. "Okay?" I ask and it's more rasp than question because it feels right to be like this, right to have her settled against me, right to have her near.

"You ask now?" she says dryly.

I shrug. "Better late than never. Now," I say tabling my question about intimacy, sensing that I need to know this just as much, if not more. "Tell me about your Gran."

And...

Claire does.

Tells me about how her next door neighbor realized something was wrong and stepped in when she didn't have to. She tells me about Gran making her feel safe and loved. Tells me how after Gran took her in, she never felt like a burden, never felt alone, never felt like she wasn't welcome.

"She sounds incredible."

"She really is," Claire agrees. "I'm lucky to have her, lucky she's had my back for as long as I can remember. I wouldn't have finished school without her, wouldn't have the job with the team if she didn't keep pushing me to be better, but—" She turns enough to meet my eyes, her front brushing against my arm. "My parents left me and had no problem doing so. Certainly, they didn't have any remorse about it," she adds dryly. "And that's not something that just goes away, even if I didn't have someone like Gran in my life. I'm thankful, *so* thankful for her, but it was hard to accept that she could love me when my parents couldn't."

"I can only imagine," I say. "Sometimes kids wonder how

their parents can love them, even if they don't give them any real reasons to think that."

"Them?" she asks. "Or you?"

I smile wryly. "We're just gonna double down on the personal on this first date?"

A dainty shrug. "Seems fitting."

It does.

Maybe that's why I don't think too hard about admitting what she already sussed out.

"Me," I admit. "Kind of difficult to not feel a little guilty when your chronic illness is the reason that your parents aren't getting sleep, or that money's tight because you broke your pump or insulin costs have gone up, or when you do something stupid as a teenager that nearly costs them everything—"

"Jackson."

"Or be the cause of their worry, even today."

Claire's hand finds mine and she laces our fingers together.

"Gran didn't have to help me," Claire says quietly. "And she gave up so much to do it. And—" Her throat works. "When she was finally going to get to enjoy her retirement, she got sick. For a long time, I felt guilty. No—" An exhale. "If I'm being completely honest, I *still* feel guilty. She gave up so much for me, and what does she have to show for it?"

"You," I say.

Her mouth kicks up. "And you don't think your parents feel the same about you?"

I know they do.

The problem is that it makes the guilt worse.

CHAPTER FIFTEEN

Claire

Shadows in his eyes.

I hate that.

I open my mouth, mind searching for something to say that will take them away, but just then, the limo slides to a halt.

He notices too.

"Enough of the heavy stuff," he murmurs, touching my cheek. "We have a first date to get to."

As though he timed it, the door swings out, momentarily blinding me from the sudden burst of sunshine. I blink, feel Jackson slide away from me.

"Come on, kitty cat," he murmurs, wrapping his big hand around mine and helping me from the car.

"Where are we—?"

But then I freeze, eyes going wide as I take in the large open field—no, not a field. It's a tarmac, dotted with futuristic-looking helicopters.

"What?" I whisper, spinning to see Jackson talking to the

limo driver. He passes the other man a folded bill, claps him on the shoulder, and then walks back to me. "How?" I ask when he comes back to my side and takes my hand again.

"I heard it all," he says, drawing me toward the office that's perched on the edge of the parking lot. "Even when I didn't want to."

Heard me tell Pru—Marcel's wife and the team's resident daredevil—that I was jealous of her adventures because I've always wanted to take a ride in a helicopter (though I had no interest in skydiving out of one like she had).

"Jackson," I whisper. Because I've heard him too.

The small things like peanut butter and jelly sandwiches forty-two minutes before game time.

And the bigger ones—about that heavy past that still weighs on him.

"Come on, kitty cat. Now's your chance for an adventure," he teases lightly. "You're not going to chicken out on me, are you?"

From this fantasy? This dream?

This chance at something I never thought I'd have?

Never.

———

"Oh my God!" I squeal—yup, squeal—as the pilot pulls up on the handle thing and takes us into the air.

I expect it to be a rush of speed and gravity like a plane, but it's smoother, quieter, especially with the heavy duty headphones covering my ears.

And the mic in front of my mouth.

Capturing my—likely—ear-piercing squeal.

"Sorry," I say, wincing at Jackson who just grins and takes my hand.

"It happens all the time," comes a calm female voice in my ears. Becky, our pilot, is confident as she navigates us higher and higher into the sky as she zooms us toward New York City.

I didn't realize we'd driven out of the city proper, not until I found myself on that tarmac, but the view back in is incredible.

Skyscrapers rise in the distance, highways dotted with hundreds of cars moving like ants form a maze in front of us. The Hudson looks grand and busy, dotted with ferries and boats. Flashes of color—green parks, silver mirrored windows, red brick buildings. It's too much to track, and yet, I can't stop taking it in.

"There's the Statue of Liberty," I gasp, interrupting our pilot as she's telling us about some of the city's history. It's interesting stuff—learning about the men who built those tall towers and the many bridges, Wall Street and the 9-11 Memorial, Central Park and the Empire State buildings. Things I may have heard or read in a history book but made more interesting.

Or maybe I'm just finally at a point in my life where I can appreciate the grandeur of this city, this experience, this…

Date.

I glance over at Jackson as Becky smoothly pivots topics and starts discussing the sister statue in Paris and how it's meant to represent the Roman goddess, Libertas. He's listening, but he's also watching me, studying me, taking in those small details.

"Thank you," I mouth, hoping he knows how much this means to me.

His eyes warm and I think…

Maybe he does.

"And she's struck by lightning about six hundred times per year—"

My eyes go wide and I focus back on Becky. "Six *hundred?*"

———

My shock didn't stop with the electric facts about Lady Liberty.

It continued as the tour wrapped up and turned back, but instead of making it all the way to that tarmac in what I learned was New Jersey, we find ourselves on top of one of the tall buildings, wind buffeting all around us as Becky pulls open the door for us and deposits us inside before waving goodbye and disappearing back into the sky.

"That was incredible," I whisper, amazed by all the noise—the motor of the helicopter, the traffic far below, the wind blowing intensely.

It was so quiet in the air, watching the world go on below us.

Now I feel dropped back into the center of everything.

"Thank you," I add, stepping close and rising on tiptoe to press a kiss to his cheek. "This was literally the best first date ever."

Furrowed brows for half a second before a cocky smile graces that handsome face and he bends, dropping his lips to mine, and allowing me to taste his happiness. "It's not even remotely over."

———

"I—"

I'm in overwhelm. I can't help it.

Helicopters. A fancy brunch. A tour of an exhibit in The Met. A walk through Central Park. Lunch from a tiny, hole-in-the-wall pizza joint with the crispiest—and most delicious— slice of margherita I've ever had the pleasure of eating.

A sunset boat tour of the Hudson with fancy cocktails.

And the whole time…

I had Jackson—the funny, nice one I saw him give to his friends and the kind, thoughtful one who knew my favorite drink, remembered my dream of riding in a helicopter. The Jackson I fantasized about.

The Jackson who's giving me a memory I know I'll always hold tight to.

And now—

I'm being led between tables in a packed but shadowy restaurant, heading toward the swinging wooden door, and—

Finding our table, right there in the kitchen.

Chefs and line cooks bustle around, clipped-out orders ringing through the space that smells like heaven.

"Too much?" Jackson asks quietly, settling his hand on the small of my back—giving me that too. The soft touches and quiet check-ins. His body coming close, his scent in my nose, his heat against my skin.

This *is* too much—him being close, the way it makes my nerves prickle at the contact. The tingle and zip around under my skin even after I lie and shake my head, still not wanting him to stop touching me. The dampness between my legs, the flutters in my belly, the way my body wants to drift closer anytime he's near.

It's almost overwhelming.

And…it's not nearly enough.

He pulls out my chair and I sink down into it, lifting up slightly as he pushes it in until I'm a reasonable distance away from my cutlery. "Good?"

I nod, finding that my mouth doesn't want to work, that my tongue doesn't seem able to form words.

A brush of his thumb along my bottom lip. "Beautiful," he murmurs. "All the time, but especially in candlelight."

Words are impossible still.

But he doesn't wait for me to stammer my way through some.

He just brushes his thumb along my bottom lip again and then rounds the table, sitting in his own chair.

"Wine?" a server asks, appearing at my elbow.

Jackson's eyes come to mine. "Pinot?"

I inhale sharply enough that my lungs protest.

He knows that too.

Knows everything and—

The day. The wonderful details and conversations that flowed naturally. The touches and smiles and—

My desperation.

My need.

It's almost pathetic.

This man could tell me we were going to run through the restaurant naked and I'd happily strip down.

This man could ask me to his bed, and I'd gleefully jump between the sheets.

This man could—

"Yes," I rasp, shoving that thought down.

But the words don't want to *stay* down.

This man could hurt me.

He nods at the waiter and thankfully, the other man disappears, leaving me to only face Jackson as I try to snap a lid on my panic attack. I'm overwhelmed because today has been out of a dream.

That's all.

It's not because I feel vulnerable and open and fucking terrified that this shit is going to burst and disappear like an over-filled balloon, gone as quickly as it appeared.

It's not.

It's. *Not*—

"Excuse me." I pop up to my feet so quickly that I almost tip my seat over backward.

"Kitty cat?"

"I'm fine," I manage to push out. "I— Bathroom—"

Where I can panic in private.

But I run out of steam there, so I just spin on my heel, hurry to the swinging doors, and push out into the dining room.

CHAPTER SIXTEEN

Jackson

I'm on my feet and following her before the door has the chance to swing closed.

Which means I nearly take off the waiter's head as I plow through.

He has a bottle in his hand—of fucking pinot grigio, just like what I ordered all of a minute ago—and I almost knock him and the expensive as fuck wine down.

Because I got the good shit.

Because Claire deserves the good shit.

And now she's hurrying through the dining room, taking a sharp left, and disappearing from sight.

Shit.

"We'll be right back," I mutter to him and race after her, turning the corner and catching a glimpse of blond hair just before a door slams shut behind her.

I reach for the knob, twisting it and pushing it open an inch.

I hear her gasp but keep nudging it inward, carefully so I don't hit her. "Just me," I murmur.

"I—"

But, by then, the door's wide enough for me to slip inside, to see—

"What the fuck?" I breathe.

To see Claire hunched in the corner, her hands over her ears. "I'm fine," she says as her knees give way and she sinks into a crouch, a tiny ball of huddled human. "I'm fine. I just need—"

Not fine.

She's so not fine.

And maybe I should wait, maybe I should give her space.

But...

I can't.

I need to touch her, to hold her, to make sure she knows she's safe.

So, I move toward her, scoop her up, and carry her to the counter next to the sink, thankful that this restaurant is expensive as shit and so it's clean. Then I reach to the door, make sure it's shut, it's locked—so no dumbass can barge in like I did.

"I'm fine," she says again as I turn back to her, and I don't bother to dignify that with a response, don't bother to do anything but move to her again, but wrap her in my arms, planting a hand in the center of her back, and drawing her to me.

"Bullshit," I say, able to feel her trembling. "You're a beautiful liar, but you're still a liar. Tell me what prompted the sprint to the bathroom. Because it sure as shit isn't an upset stomach."

Silence.

Then a stunned blip of laughter.

"No," she admits with a long, shuddering exhale. "It's not

an upset stomach." Another breath and then she pushes lightly at my chest.

I drop my arms.

I don't want to, but I hear it in her voice. The strength returning. Her spine straightening. Knowing whatever threw her is being pushed aside.

"Gonna clue me in?" I ask, and yeah, it's less a request and more an order, but…I said what I said.

"No," she says, shoving my chest, pushing me backward, and she says it so matter-of-factly that the word takes me a moment to process.

In that moment, she's moving toward the door.

I catch her arm, draw her back, dragging her hand away from the knob. "Nice try, kitty cat." I spin her in my hold, pin her in place with my gaze.

"Are you going to tell me about what I found out?" she whispers. "And why it made you hate me?"

A cold-ass bucket of water over my head.

My hand drops to my side.

Her smile is small and…sad.

"Fuck, I—"

"No," she says, guilt intruding in on her expression. "I'm being a jerk. I—" She takes a breath. "I'm sorry. I guess…I guess I'm still struggling with this— After my date—"

Rage in my belly. "That guy was a dick—"

"It's not him—" She presses her lips together. "Okay, so it's not *all* about him. I can't lie, him taking a look at me and GTFOing freaking stings, but I…" A sigh. "That's not why I—"

"Why you ran away from wine?"

"You know I like pinot grigio," she murmurs.

I touch her cheek, heart squeezing. "I pay attention, and so do you."

She drops her chin to her chest. "Yes, but…"

"What?"

"I just keep waiting for the bubble to burst. Like"—she throws up her hands and exhales, pacing away—"how is this real life? It's got to be a dream, and I'm going wake up again and you're not there and—"

"You're going to wake up and I'm not there?"

She flushes.

"Kitty cat," I say silkily, snaking a hand around her middle and drawing her flush against me. "Do you have something to tell me?"

"You mean besides the fact that this day has been fucking perfect and I can't believe it's real and I'm scared that I'll never have anything to compare with it ever again?" she asks, her tone tart, her palm pressing to my chest.

Trying to escape. To avoid. To prevaricate.

But I won't let her.

No fucking way.

"You'll have something to compare it to." Lots of some-things, because I'll make sure of it.

"I—"

"You'll wake up and *I* won't be there?"

Bright red cheeks. Teeth pressed into her bottom lip. Eyes that are slipping away from mine. "I dream about you sometimes."

I grin. I shouldn't but...

"Is that all?"

Her cheeks grow brighter. "Y-yes?"

"Kitty cat," I warn.

Her chin lifts. "Fine," she snaps, "I've dreamed about you and thought about you and used my vibrator to make myself come to those thoughts and dreams, okay?" She tosses up her hands. "Is that a crime?"

"No, sweetheart," I tell her, drawing her closer, tracing a finger over the flush on her cheeks, one at a time. "It's just something I'm now desperate to see."

"O-oh," she whispers, and I can feel her trembling, can see the desire creep into those pretty brown eyes. "Do—"

"Do I what?" I ask, dick twitching, desire making my hands shake as I tuck her hair behind her ears, as I stroke a finger along her throat. I want to lift her back onto the counter, want to kiss and touch her until she comes. Want to tease those fantasies out of her and diligently act out each and every one.

But this is her first date. *Ever.*

And we're in a bathroom.

And we have a chef waiting to serve us an amazing fucking meal.

I want her to have everything she's ever wanted. I want to spoil her, treat her with such fucking care that she doesn't question it, that she expects it from the men in her life.

Men in her life.

The thought makes my blood boil.

But I shove that down, clamp a lid onto the jealously, the rage at the thought of another man touching, stroking, *loving* her.

"I'm here because I want to be," I tell her. "I'm here because I'm lucky enough that you agreed to let me take you out. I'm here because"—I cup her jaw, tilt her head up so our gazes are aligned—"you're wonderful, kitty cat, and I'm desperate to spend time with you, as little or as much as you'll give me."

I get to watch the beauty that appears in her eyes at my words.

Not the disbelief from when we talked in that empty room.

Not the edge of surprise and uncertainty that's been clinging to her irises all day long.

Not the hurt from my sharp words and asshole behavior, doing my fucking best to push her away.

This is...

As though I've peeled the layers back and managed a glimpse of the woman beneath.

A confident, beautiful woman who's maybe finally begun to understand how truly wonderful she is.

A gorgeous, sexy woman who trails a hand down my chest, allows her body to sink against mine.

A stunning, amazing woman who shocks the shit out of me by grabbing two fistfuls of my hair and...

Kissing me senseless.

CHAPTER SEVENTEEN

Claire

I...

Well, fuck it.

Has my life pivoted on its ear in the last twenty-four hours?

Yup.

Am I ready to start rolling with it?

Also...

Yup.

Which is why I stop listening to the voices in my head, grab two fistfuls of Jackson's hair, and bring my mouth to his.

All day he's been so close. All day I've wanted to touch him, to taste him, to feel this.

A spark turning into flames.

My body instantly tap-dancing on the edge of control, flaring with heat and need and the understanding that I'm desperate for something I've never experienced anywhere but my bedroom—alone.

I want Jackson's hard body pressing me into my mattress, want his rough hands stroking over my skin, want him pushing inside me and—

He tears his mouth from mine, chest heaving, eyes burning, hands on my waist. "Really, kitty cat?"

My lips are tingling, along with every nerve in my body, it seems. "I'm desperate to spend time with you too."

Silence falls between us—tense and filled with emotion and then he's groaning and wrapping his arms around me, dropping his mouth to mine, kissing me until I can't breathe, can't think, can't do anything but hold on...

And kiss him back.

Knock. Knock. *Knock!*

He freezes, growl rumbling up the back of his throat, teasing along my tongue, vibrating against my chest, sensitizing my nipples and making me want to seal my mouth to his all over again.

In fact, I almost give in to the urge to do just that when—

Knock. Knock. *Knock!*

"Sir," a voice echoes through the wood and it takes me a moment to place it, to remember that we were sitting down for dinner before I freaked out, ran off, and accosted my date in the bathroom.

Oh, God. We're making out in the bathroom of an extremely fancy New York City restaurant and—

"Is everything okay in there?"

"It fucking isn't," Jackson mutters, glancing down and I follow his gaze, mouth dropping open at the—

"Is that your penis?" I exclaim softly.

"Yup."

"It's huge," I say, genuinely aghast.

"The tent I'm sporting makes it look bigger than it is," he says and the anger's gone from his voice. Instead, there's amusement and humor and...

Heat.

"It'll fit, kitty cat," he murmurs, sealing his lips to mine for a brief, scorching kiss. "I promise."

"How?" I ask, even though I know logically he's telling me the truth. People have sex all the time and my toys—

His rough chuckle shouldn't gather between my legs, should have me wanting to be back in my hotel room, draining the battery of my vibrator and—

"Hold that thought," he mutters, dropping his head again, flicking his tongue over the expanse of my throat, nipping lightly with his teeth. "Because, fuck, I need to know exactly what it was that put that look in your eyes."

"I—"

But he presses his thumb to my bottom lip, spins us both to the door, wrenching it open as the waiter knocks again. "Hey," he says. "We'll take that pinot now."

Then he's guiding me down the hall and back through the dining room, totally ignoring the fact that the waiter is gaping at us, that I'm sputtering about explaining that we weren't boning in the bathroom, that I'm—

Jackson pulls out my chair, nudges me down into it, and then settles across from me.

"Wine?" the waiter asks, making me jump.

Full circle.

I've come full circle.

And this time, I'm determined not to ruin it.

———

"And then you just roll your hands like this—" The chef, Kurt, who happens to be one of Jackson's old friends, reaches around me, his arms guiding mine as we drag the pasta dough over the specially carved wooden board.

"Oh!" I say as a perfectly formed piece of pasta emerges.

"That's so cool." Jackson growls, and I just pick up the tiny shaped noodle, grinning at him. "Isn't that amazing?"

"Amazing," he mutters, sounding very far from astonished about my noodle-crafting skills.

Especially since his gaze is not on the noodle I'm holding up, but instead is murderous and fixed on Kurt.

Who coughs and steps back, saying, "I'll let you two keep going with that. I'll finish up the sauce."

"Exactly," Jackson grumbles as he rounds the steel table and stands next to me. "Because we're supposed to be eating, not cooking."

I don't know what propels me to do it—maybe it's that commitment to this day, this dream, this date. Or maybe it's just that I pay attention to the small moments, the small things —or in this case, the *obvious* things. I rise up on tiptoe, press my lips to his stubble-covered jaw and murmur, "Kurt's cute but I prefer hockey players to chefs."

He exhales.

"And thank you for bringing me here so I can learn this."

And I get to watch the big, strong hockey player melt.

His expression is something I'll never forget, even though I only get it for a second before he's bending down and kissing me.

"Beautiful little kitty cat," he says when he draws back, lightly tapping at my nose. "Now get on with those noodles. I'm hungry."

Lips twitching, I get on with the noodles.

And so, by the time the sauce is ready and they're dropped in the water to cook, Jackson is prebolusing for dinner, giving the insulin a head start on the carbs that are soon to follow.

"Sit, sit," Kurt orders, gesturing toward the table he pulled us from when I started peppering him with questions thirty minutes before. Our waiter—who hasn't been able to meet my eyes since we came face-to-face outside the bathroom—is depositing plates in front of our chairs.

Colorful salads, crusty bread, and a beautiful array of cock-tails to accompany our wine.

"Enjoy," he adds, shooing us from the kitchen and working furiously at his station.

We sit. We devour the salads, and I definitely have more than my share of the delicious bread.

And by the time my head is spinning slightly from the rainbow of cocktails, from polishing that bottle of wine off—even with all the bread soaking it up in my belly—the chef is depositing steaming plates of the most delicious pasta in front of me.

But it's not just the food.

It's...Jackson.

His continued awareness and consideration, the way his hand brushes mine as we share the dishes and offer each other bites, how our legs tangle beneath the table, the soft contact always there. The stories he shares of the team's locker room antics—some I've heard, many I haven't, all that have me in stitches.

And then he asks me questions about Gran, and I find myself talking about our traditions at Christmas—Chinese food and a movie at the local theater, about Junie and the bingo fiasco, about my attempts at making her a birthday cake as a teenager and not realizing that I'd swapped salt for sugar, and about the hard times too.

"...I thought I'd lose her when the cancer came back," I admit. "I went home and cried all night, but then I did what she taught me—I got myself together, I did my research, and I made a plan. I got her doctors to get her into a clinical trial and thankfully, she responded well to it. She's still recovering, and I hate that her journey hasn't been easy, but she's getting better a little more every day. And she's been cancer free for six months now."

Jackson squeezes my hand. "She's lucky to have you."

"I feel the same."

He opens his mouth, but whatever he was going to ask is interrupted by his phone ringing.

CHAPTER EIGHTEEN

Jackson

I pull out my phone and grimace at the caller ID, weighing my options.

If I ignore this call like I've been ignoring the texts all day, my mom might do something dramatic—

Like get on a damned plane and knock on my door in the middle of the night.

And I have plans that don't involve calming my hysterical mother.

"You should get that," Claire murmurs.

I shake my head, pocketing my still vibrating phone. "Let's enjoy our dinner. I don't want to interrupt."

"Like I did with my freakout and sprint to the bathroom?"

My grin is wolfish. "Minus the freakout, I very much liked making out with you in the bathroom. Especially because you agreed to act out those fantasies you have about me."

Her eyebrows fly up, cheeks flaring bright. "Excuse me?"

My phone cuts off, and I lean across the table, brushing my

knuckles along the column of her throat...right as my phone starts up again.

Claire hears it, and she captures my hand, presses a kiss to my palm that has my cock twitching. "Answer it," she orders softly. "I'll just be here with my lemon cake."

One of the many desserts Kurt brought out.

Asshole's clearly trying to impress my girl.

The thought gives me pause—like wanting to plot the murder of an old friend— but Claire's reaching for her fork and scooping up a bite of cake, her soft moan wrapping its fingers around my cock and distracting me from the murderous thoughts.

Lucky bastard.

Saved by a moan.

"Honey?"

I blink, tearing my gaze from her lush mouth, the tip of that pink tongue flicking out to capture a bit of icing. I want it tracing along the head of my cock, dragging lower, over my balls. I want—

"Honey, are you there?"

This time the question is loud enough that I realize I've somehow answered on speaker.

Claire looks up, eyebrows dragged together, concern on her face. "You okay?" she mouths.

I was just thinking about you sucking my dick, no big deal.

"I'm here, Mom," I say before that little nugget slips out and I both scar my mother and send Claire running out of the kitchen a second time.

Though...

She picks up the fork again, brings it to her mouth—

A hint of wicked in her eyes as she dips it inside, as she allows her lips to drag along the tines, capturing the thick, white frosting and swallowing it with a soft moan.

I'm hard.

I've been in a perpetual state of arousal from the moment I

first saw Claire, and it hasn't eased over the years. And after having tasted her, touched her, learned more about her, peeled back the layers to get to know the wonderful woman beneath…that's only grown.

Until I want to fuck her here on the table or back in that bathroom.

But…control.

Slow and steady, showing her how fucking great she is.

Not taking advantage of a virgin because my dick is hard.

"…and then your dad said—"

I shake myself, not missing the sly little smile Claire sends me, not missing that the tiny smirk tells me far more than anything else today. She's getting more confident, more comfortable.

This is working.

I tamp down on my arousal, focus in on my mom—and apparently the story of their neighbor ripping down one of their exterior cameras. Because pRiVaCy! Even though it wasn't pointing at their neighbor's property but instead down into the back yard so they could keep an eye on Fluffy, my parents' elderly pooch.

"—and then Todd said…"

My brows shoot up and a bolt of anger ricochets through me. "What the fuck, Mom? I'm calling your attorney. Right now. He can't threaten you like that."

"Don't worry, honey. I was recording and called the police, and Todd's daughter has had enough of his shit so he's spending the next few days in jail."

"And what happens when he gets out?" I mutter.

"I can handle a grumpy, eighty-year-old man—"

"Because she's married to one!" my dad calls, sounding far too fucking chipper for having dealt with their insane neighbor.

"You're not eighty, baby—ha, that rhymes."

"No, that's a slant rhyme because it's close but not truly—"

"Mom," I grit out.

"I can handle Todd," she says. "And it helps that his daughter is on our side. She's had enough of him terrorizing the neighborhood, so she's moving him into a home and selling the house to pay for it."

"But—"

"Don't feel bad for him," she goes on with barely a breath. "You remember Jenny from the other side of the road?"

"Yeah," I say carefully.

"He poured bleach on her lawn because he didn't like that her kids were playing out front so much."

"Oh, my God."

Except that's not me talking.

Claire clamps a hand to her mouth, wincing. "Sorry," she whispers, dropping it a second later.

"Is that a woman?" my mother trills.

Claire winces again.

"Yeah, Mom," I say. "That's why I wasn't picking up the phone."

"Because you're on a *date*," she says slowly.

"Mom," I warn.

"Your son is on a date!" she hollers at my dad.

"A date?" my dad shouts, making me hold the phone away from my ear.

Claire giggles.

I sigh.

"We'll let you get back to your *date*," she says archly, making me groan, but before she hangs up, she calls, loud enough that I know Claire can hear it clear as day, "Nice to meet you Mystery Date. I hope we'll get to chat soon!"

"Mom—"

"My name is Claire," she says. "And I'm sure we'll talk soon."

"Claire?" my dad's voice echoes through the speakers. "*The* Claire?"

Shit.

"Bye, guys. Love you. Talk soon," I say in a hurry then shove my phone in my pocket.

Silence falls between us.

Then her lips twitch. "Your parents are great."

I groan. "They meddle and drive me batshit crazy," I grumble, rubbing at a throb in my temple. "But, yeah," I admit. "They're great."

"The Claire?"

"I might have mentioned you a time." A beat. "Or a hundred."

Her face softens. "Just so you know, Gran knows all about you." She smiles. "And regularly gives me a hard time about it —but I still think she's awesome."

"She loves you."

"Yeah," she whispers.

"Want to call her too?" I joke. "Get her to bellow into the phone speaker, just for funsies?"

She grins. "Gran is less of a bellower than your parents, but I'm sure she could be up for the challenge."

I laugh, reach over to pick up her fork and steal a bite of cake. "Christ, that's good," I moan. "Even though Kurt is an asshole."

"I thought he was your friend?"

"Not anymore."

She looks from the plates to the kitchen then back to me. "Is there a reason?"

"Yeah," I grumble, stealing one more bite before handing her the fork back. The asshole can cook, I'll give Kurt that much. "He touched you."

Her lips twitch and then she opens her mouth.

But fucking Kurt comes out right then.

"Try this," he says, depositing a plate in front of Claire.

"I couldn't possibly—" But she picks up her fork anyway, dipping it into the concoction Kurt brought and moaning.

My friend—*ex* friend—smirks at me and it takes everything in me to not reach across the table and throttle him.

But I don't.

Instead, I get up, lift her from the chair, sit my ass down in it, and then draw her into my lap. "Fuck off," I tell Kurt.

Who just grins.

Raises his hands.

And then walks away.

Leaving us alone.

Fucking finally.

CHAPTER NINETEEN

Claire

My heart is still beating from the way he lifted me up and deposited me into his lap, from that show of strength and how he didn't give a fuck that people might see.

From the gentle way he fed me the petite dessert I should have been too full to eat, but somehow found the space for.

He refused to let me even finish my offer of paying for dinner and then bundled me into my coat, took my hand, grunted his thanks at Kurt (and passed a folded bill to our poor, innocent and now emotionally scarred waiter), and then led me out onto the sidewalk.

We've been all over the city today—but the path he'd taken us on was well thought out and flowed.

Case in point?

Only needing to walk a couple of blocks back to our hotel.

"Cold?" he asks as the wind picks up, tucking me closer before I can tell him that I'm fine.

But since I like being here—cuddled against his warm strength, his arm wrapped tightly around me, I don't protest.

"Tell me about your diabetes," I say. His chest inflates and the pause is so long that I find myself adding, "I mean, I know the basics, but I just…I'd like to know the day-to-day stuff."

I want to know how it affects his life, how I can make it easier for him.

Want to know the little things so that his plate isn't so full.

"Or not," I say when he doesn't reply. "It's okay to not want to talk about it. I know I'm being pushy—"

"No." He touches my cheek. "It's strange because it's my entire life and it's not—or that's always what my parents wanted for me. For it to not stop me from doing what I want. And it hasn't. I'm here. I'm far more affected by what happened when I was in high school—"

I suck in a breath.

The incident that made him hate me. The incident that made him hate himself.

But he keeps talking and because I'm desperate to know every part of him, I push down any questions and just listen.

"—than I am from diabetes. Has it fucked with my life in a multitude of ways? Yup. Of course it has. I have to wait to eat what I want sometimes. Have to eat when I'm not hungry other times. I'm not supposed to be too low because I might, you know, die, but I also can't allow my glucose to trend too high because I might, you know, die, albeit more slowly. I've heard the jokes about eating too much sugar, heard the whispers about how unhealthy my diet must be, heard the judgments about how I'm managing my diet."

I wrap my arm around his waist, needing to hug him, needing him to know I'm here.

"I've listened to the comments about being on my phone all the time, when I need it because it's my fucking medical device. I've put up with bullshit comments about my pump or CGM beeping. I've dealt with all of the not fun stuff that comes from having an invisible, lifelong illness," he says, drawing me even closer. "But so have so many other people. If anything, it's been far less of *why me* and far more of giving me an understanding that we all have these challenges we're dealing with, so we need to bring more empathy and understanding into this world."

"That's why you have the charity?"

He works with local kids who have health challenges.

"Why not me?" He shrugs. "I have the money, and it's important enough to make the time."

"And yet, you still don't recognize how wonderful you are?"

"Kitty cat," he begins, and it's dark but the glittering lights of NYC mean that I can see the disbelief in his eyes.

"Don't." I turn further into his side, lifting up on tiptoe so I can cup both sides of his face. "All day you've been telling me to accept that you're doing this for me because you like me, because I'm a good person with a good heart, because I deserve it."

He opens his mouth, but I keep going.

"And so, you can't do all of that, *say* all of that, show me that reality, and expect me to just keep accepting the awful bullshit you spew."

"Claire."

"Because it *is* bullshit, bullshit you use to keep yourself distant from the world, to keep your heart and soul safe. If you don't ever let anyone all the way in, they can't hurt you—"

"I tried that before."

"I know, honey," I whisper. "And I know it went bad."'

Pain and anger in his eyes. "Bad?" he says quietly. "Bad, kitty cat? I nearly killed someone. I put them in the hospital for months and months."

The middle of the street is far from the place for this conversation.

But...

I find I can't let it go.

"You hurt them because they raped your girlfriend."

His big body shudders.

"I know I shouldn't have seen the files," I murmur. "And I didn't even mean to look. But I was helping the social worker who was on my case move offices—"

"Of course you were."

"And I saw your name in the files." Guilt threads itself through my belly again. "I wish I could lie and say I dropped the box and the papers just happened to be right there, but that's not what happened." I sigh. "I saw your name. I snooped because I thought you might be hiding something that could hurt the team. And I found a painful part of your past you wanted to forget." I suck in a breath, release it slowly. "I really am sorry."

He smooths a hand over the back of my head, calloused palm catching on the strands of my hair. "I know you are."

"But I'm also not," I admit. "Because I know that deep dark secret of yours, know exactly why you keep beating yourself up over and over again for it. And I know that you're not the bad person you think you are."

"Claire, if this comes out, my position in the league—"

"You think that Luc doesn't know already?"

He rocks back on his toes, eyes going wide.

But I don't miss the anger in them.

The hurt.

The panic.

"You told him?"

I shake my head. "Of course not. "But the news stories are out there and the social media posts and...if someone wanted to look, wanted to talk about it, they would."

"Those records are sealed." He shudders. "That can't be right. I—"

"I'm not saying that the guys or even Luc or Lexi know what happened—" Though I'd bet he does because Luc is... Luc. He knows all, and he and his wife and team lawyer, Lexi, have ways to dig out all the skeletons that might come back to hurt the team. And my bet would be on Smitty knowing too, considering how gently he handles Jackson—

Though who knows?

I've been wrong about so much.

"I'm just saying," I go on, "that if it all came out, your friends would still be your friends. Your past wouldn't change how they look at you, nor the respect they carry for you. They'd know that you protected a person you loved, that you accepted the consequences that came from that, and then you moved on and made something wonderful with your life."

He's quiet and statue-still for a long, *long* moment. Then he drops his chin, settling it on the top of my head. "How can you be so sure?"

I inhale, hold it for a long moment.

Then exhale softly. "Because I know *you*."

"The guy who was an asshole?"

I wrap both arms around his middle, press my body to his. "No. The man who felt something for me and did everything in his power to keep me away so I wouldn't get hurt."

A quiet curse. "Dammit, kitty cat."

"Dammit because you know I'm right? Because you know they'd do the same exact thing if they were in your situation? Because you were scared and maybe still are scared? Because I sure as hell am scared that all these big feelings I have for you might end up not being enough, might leave us both wounded and alone."

"Claire—"

"But I'm done with letting that rule me. I spent years on the sidelines of my life before I found the courage to try, and you know what?"

A long blip of quiet before his arms tighten and his head lifts, and thank God, but the humor is back in his eyes. "What?"

"Smitty gives great advice."

"Heaven help me," he mutters then exhales. "Lay it on me."

"Practice makes perfect."

Laughter rumbles up and out of his chest, filling the air between us. "Fuck me," he says. "But the asshole is right."

"Smitty's not an ass—"

But before I can finish that thought, he's yanking me even closer, bending, and…

Showing me that practicing making out with a hot hockey player is fun as hell.

"Get a room, yeah?" someone bellows from behind us, making me jump and us break apart.

Jackson sighs and settles his forehead against mine, mouth curved up at the edges. "Speaking of rooms," he says. "Come on, kitty cat. Let's get you back to yours."

CHAPTER TWENTY

Jackson

I lean in and press my mouth to hers, resisting the urge to deepen the kiss, but only just barely.

It would be so easy to nudge that door open, to talk my way inside.

But this is her first date ever.

She only had her first kiss yesterday.

Slow. Patient.

Make her see.

But…

She's the one opening my eyes, dropping fucking truth bombs on me that have me reconsidering everything I've held as truth over the last decade.

"Good night, kitty cat."

"Night," she murmurs but she doesn't step inside her room and close the door as I expect, as I need her to do to keep my fraying self-control intact.

"What?" I ask when she studies me.

"Why do you call me that?"

I sidle a little closer, intending to steal one more kiss before nudging her inside and slamming the door closed behind her…with me on this side and her safely in her room. "Hmm?"

"Why do you call me kitty cat?"

My eyes flick up to hers, and fuck it, I just give her the truth. "Because I've been obsessed with your pussy from day one."

Silence.

Her mouth dropping open. "Seriously?" she whispers.

I shrug. "You want me to lie to you?"

"N-no," she sputters, cheeks blazing. "I just—"

I lean in, whispering in her ear, inhaling the soft floral scent of her. "You're not the only one with fantasies, remember?"

Her throat works. "I remember." A breath, her hand settling on my chest, dragging lower. "Come in."

I nearly groan, but bite it back, force my hands to release her. "Not tonight, sweetheart. We've already moved at warp speed."

Enemies to first date in the span of a day.

I need that patience, need to make sure she moves at a pace she's comfortable with.

"Just for a little while," she murmurs, slipping that palm down a little lower, until her fingers are positioned just above the waistband of my slacks.

My dick is hard—just like that.

"Please?"

And, fuck, but I can't say no, can't find the strength within myself to give her anything but *everything* she wants.

I capture her hand, bring it up to my lips, pressing a kiss to the center of her palm, and the disappointment that enters her gaze—like she knows I'm going to say no, like she expects it—takes any angst out of the decision.

It took courage for her to make the request.

Fuck if I'm going to shit on that.

I nudge her backward, beyond the door, catching the heavy

panel before it can slam and disturb our neighbors. I don't want any interruptions. I don't want any nosy teammates—cough Smitty—who I know is likely nearby, ready to snoop and gather gossip to barge in and—

"You can go to your own room," she whispers, and I realize I've been staring at the closed door for far too long. "I didn't mean to pressure you."

I throw the deadbolt, whip around.

"I'm trying not to toss you on the bed and fuck you senseless."

Her lips part. Her cheeks flush. Her eyes darken. "Oh, I—"

"But you've just had your first date, after only just having your first kiss, after dealing with a bunch of assholes. You're not ready—"

"Yes, I am," she says quickly, her tongue dipping out to taste her bottom lip. "I'm ready. I want—" Her teeth press into her bottom lip for a brief second. "I need—" She reaches for the buttons of her coat, undoing it and dropping it onto the chair in the corner of the room. The movement means that her jeans—already sinfully tight—lovingly cup that gorgeous ass of hers, that her silky shirt stretches tightly over her breasts.

I want to see—no, I'm fucking desperate to see what she's wearing beneath her clothes.

Christ.

It's a fucking miracle that there's any blood left in my brain.

It's sure as shit is pooling in my groin, making all my thoughts of *patience* and *slow* very hard to grasp on to.

"You need what?" I rasp when she turns her back on me, resting her hands on the dresser, dropping her chin to her chest.

"I don't know," she admits a long moment later.

Only the way she says that…

"Liar," I accuse softly. "Beautiful, beautiful liar."

A sharp exhale. "Fine," she says on another sigh, spinning

to face me. "You want the truth? My skin's on fire," she adds before I can say yes, I want that, almost as much as I want *her*. "I want to tear off your clothes, to feel every part of you against me, to have you pressing me into the mattress and kissing every inch of me and giving me an orgasm. I'm so wet that I feel like the barest touch from you is going to make me spontaneously combust and—" She shakes her head. "I've waited twenty-five years for this. I'm fucking tired of standing on the sidelines of my life, watching the years pass by too scared to go after what I want or too intent on keeping people at a distance. I want a future that's full. I want a life that's filled with pleasure and pain and everything in between."

My control snaps.

I close the distance between us in an instant and scoop her up, dumping her on the bed in a rush that sends the air rushing out of her lungs.

"Jackson!" she exclaims when I yank off one shoe and then the other, tossing them over my shoulder, not giving a fuck where they land.

"You—"

I climb up next to her, sealing my mouth over hers, plunging one hand into her hair, the other clamping to her waist and drawing her against me, beneath me.

Her nails bite into my arms and there's no teaching required when one of her legs settles around my waist, heel digging into my butt.

Instinct.

Two bodies learning each other—*knowing* each other.

I drag my mouth along her jaw, nibble at her earlobe, taste the slender column of her throat.

She's grinding against me, the sexiest little moans filling the air, her hips finding a rhythm that's slowly driving me insane—and we're barely even started. "Oh, God," she whispers when I flick open the top button on her blouse, when I taste the silken skin between her collarbones.

"Too much?"

A shake of her head. "Not enough."

Grinning, I continue slowly unbuttoning her shirt, method-ically tasting the flesh I expose, parting the material, coaxing her up so I can free it from her body.

She trembles, and I realize I'm staring. "Fucking beautiful," I murmur.

She is—outside and in, from the tips of her pale pink painted toes to the soft blond of her hair. And all the curves in between. Slowly, I trail my hand up her side, tracing the flare of her hip, the curve of her waist, stopping just beneath her breasts.

"Yes," she whispers.

I'm shaking as I slide my hand up, cupping her over the plain cotton bra, feeling the tight bead of her nipple against my palm. I watch her face as I touch her, committing to memory what makes her lips part in pleasure, her hips buck against mine, her color heighten. But I don't want it to just be me paying attention, clocking those details, know it *can't* be only me, not if it's going to be everything *she* needs. "I do something you don't like," I say, waiting for her eyes to come to mine, making sure she sees how serious I am. "You tell me, and we'll stop. I don't care if I'm balls deep, okay?"

"I—" Teeth in her bottom lip.

"I need you to make that promise for me, okay?"

She inhales. Exhales. Then nods. "If I don't like something I'll tell you."

"And we'll stop," I say again.

Another nod. "Yes," she says, tone going firm. "We'll stop, so long as you agree to tell me if I do something *you* don't like."

"Not possible, kitty cat."

"I think it is—"

I nip at her bottom lip. "You're not even touching me and I'm ready to explode. This is your first time," I remind her, ignoring the pink cheeks, "you need to feel like you're in control."

She wraps her hand around my wrist. "Then touch me, Jackson. Stroke my breasts and pinch my nipples the way I've imagined you doing a hundred times before. Slip your hand into my underwear and tease my clit. Fuck me with your fingers and suck my breasts and—"

Red hazes at the edges of my vision as the rest of my control snaps.

I undo her bra with a flick of my fingers and then I'm palming the lush globes, rolling the beaded nipples between thumb and forefinger.

She moans, her head falling back on the pillows. "Oh, God."

I keep going, adding my mouth, skipping forward a few items on her list because I need to worship those breasts, because she orders, "More."

So, I give her more.

I taste and nip, squeeze and stroke, and then I'm shifting my weight so I can snake one hand down and slip my hand beneath the waistband of her jeans.

A sharp breath that has me pausing...

And her grabbing my wrist, guiding me down, coaxing me to flick open the button on her jeans and slipping my fingers into the slick folds between her legs.

"Fuck, I can't wait to taste this slick pussy."

Her lips part, and then I'm gently stroking her, watching for any discomfort, testing pressure and angle, circles and strokes. Her flush spreads down along her throat, over the tops of her breasts. Her hips start the rhythm again, as though seeking purchase. I give it to her—on her clit, circling her entrance, sliding the tip of my finger into her sopping cunt. She goes still. "Jackson."

Immediately, I freeze. "Too much?"

"God, no," she whispers, chest heaving. "That—" A shake of her head. "Your finger and your thumb...I—"

"You what?" I ask, starting up again.

"I'm going to come if you keep doing that."

A rush of blood to my groin, my vision growing even hazier, my cock even harder, but I don't stop my finger and thumb, don't fuck with that rhythm. I keep going, leaning down to suck a nipple deep, slipping a second finger inside when she softens, allowing me in, knowing she'll need more to take me, knowing she fucking loves it by the tremor that ricochets through her body, knowing it from my name on her tongue, her hands in my hair, her pussy clamping hard around my fingers.

"Oh God. Oh God. Oh—"

She freezes and I feel it—the gush of her desire as her orgasm races through her.

I keep stroking, keep kissing, keep guiding her through until she goes limp beneath me, slumping against the mattress.

"Claire?" I murmur, lifting my head, my dick rock-hard, my vision hazy, my hands shaking as I reach for her jeans, ready to tear them free and thrust home. "You good?"

Then I hear it.

The soft snore.

My gaze flies to her face and...

Disappointment wars with tenderness.

I don't know if it's the food or the drinks or the long day, but her eyes are closed, her body is lax, and her mouth is slightly parted as her breaths come slow and steady, slow and steady.

She's sleeping.

Christ.

While my dick is ready to break in half and I'm ridiculously close to an orgasm.

But she's also...trusting me.

Feeling safe enough to fall asleep here, like this.

Something settles in my chest—a wound closing or maybe hooks sinking deeper.

I can't tell for sure, but it's an acute type of pain, the best type of pain—aching muscles after a long workout, scoring a goal despite getting slashed...pushing through discomfort and finding something beautiful on the other side.

So, I hold tight to that pain, tuck it close as I bring the covers up and over us—

And let sleep take me under.

CHAPTER TWENTY-ONE

Claire

I'm hot.

Scorching and sweaty, like the time I fell asleep in Gran's garden in the hell of a humid summer day, waking up sunburned and dripping with perspiration, ready to pass out.

I'd stumbled into the house, gulped down water, allowed the air conditioning to sweep over me, the cool blast beneath the vent enough to bring my temperature down.

But there's no relief now.

Slowly, I peel my lids back, realize that the inferno isn't the sun blasting down on me.

It's in the form of a strong body pressed close to my back, arms holding me tight, warm, damp breath on the back of my neck.

This was one of my fantasies too—waking up with Jackson in my bed, his body wrapped around mine...

Just without the side of sweat.

My mouth curving, I poke a foot out, feel the cool air of the hotel room ghosting over my skin, an instant relief that has me realizing that while I'm a little sweaty, I'm not nearly as bad off as that day all those summers ago.

But geez, how does a human make this much heat?

I shift forward, seeking more coolness, drawing the blanket off my legs.

I'm wearing my jeans. No wonder it's hot as fuck. Of course, I *am* topless so one would think that would counteract some of the heat.

Not so much, apparently—

Wait.

I'm *topless*.

As in, last thing I remember, Jackson was worshiping my body, giving me an orgasm that was so fucking all-consuming that I forgot what my name was and where I was and—

Well, I wasn't doing much thinking.

I was feeling and I was…

Oh, my God.

I whip my head around, get a glimpse of Jackson's sleeping form. *His fully clothed* sleeping form.

Shit.

"I fell asleep!"

I don't realize I said that out loud until his eyes slowly open—

Fuzzy with sleep, his expression is adorable, and he looks like he's about ten years younger, like the little boy who protected his girlfriend and lost so much and—

He rumbles out a groan, wrapping his arm tighter around my middle and rolling us until I'm pinned beneath him. "You fell asleep on me," he mutters, nipping at the bottom side of my jaw.

"I know," I say softly, not wanting to ruin the hush of the morning, the quiet peace that's surrounding us. Soon enough he'll have to get up for morning skate, get ready for the game tonight, "I'm sorry. I guess I ate or drank too much."

His lips find mine for a blazing kiss before he smirks down

at me. "Either that or your man gave you an orgasm that made you all but pass out."

He sounds cocky.

And I guess he earned that cockiness.

Because he's right—the last thing I remember is pleasure spiraling through my veins, sending me to the stratosphere and then...

Heat.

He kisses the tip of my nose, smile softening, eyes warm. "Don't worry about it, kitty cat," he says gently, rightly reading the guilt in my eyes at ending something I pushed for because I fell asleep, at getting pleasure while he was left unsatisfied. "I say it's my fault for dragging you all over the city yesterday."

My mouth curves. "It was a great day, though."

"The best," he agrees. "Though..."

"What?" Curiosity courses through me...along with heat because his expression is nothing short of wicked.

"Maybe we can make today better." He trails a hand up my side, drifting his fingers along the underside of my breast.

I shiver. "I think we can."

"Mmm." He drags his mouth down my neck, along my collar bones, toward my breast, and his lips are just sealing around my nipple when my cell rings.

He freezes, hot breath on my flesh.

"Ignore it," I say, arching up, offering my breast, all but begging him to suck.

He does—

For one brief moment.

But then my lifts his head, reaching over me for my phone. "Can't concentrate with that shit—"

"It's okay," I tell him. "I'll turn it off and—" I'm reaching too, and our hands and arms connect and—

Somehow, I swipe across the screen.

Answering the call.

No.

Answering the *video* call.

Gran's face appears on the screen. "Morning, honey. I—*Oh, my God!*"

"*Oh, my God!*" I shriek remembering that I'm fucking topless and leaning over my phone screen and—

"Fuck," Jackson mutters, yanking the blankets over me before extracting himself and taking the phone, turning it toward himself instead of leaving it pointed at me in my topless state.

"Who are you?" Gran asks sharply.

"Jackson," he says. "Jackson Hunter. I'm—" His eyes come to mine, and I hold my breath, wondering what he's going to say.

I'm his *what?*

Date? Hookup? Is he going to take this chance to put distance between us?

"Claire's boyfriend," he says quietly, his gaze flicking back to the phone screen.

I—

What?

But also...*squee?*

"The Jackson from the team?" Gran asks, tone still sharp, but softening now because I've talked about him—the good things. Not our taut relationship over the last months, but the things I knew of him before, the things I know of him now.

The charity. How hard he works. What a good friend and teammate he is.

"Hmm," she says and her tone is like steel when she orders, "Give the phone to my granddaughter and step out of the room please."

I gulp, audibly apparently, if the amused look that Jackson tosses my way is any indication, but I snag my cell when he passes it over. "Hi, Gran," I say carefully.

"Is he gone?"

The bathroom door clicks closed.

I nod.

"You're safe?"

I nod a second time.

"And happy?"

I bite my lip and nod again.

Her expression gentles, relief in her eyes, and then she smiles. "Tell me all about it."

And...so I do.

———

"Are you sure about this?" I ask thirty minutes later after we've showered—Jackson doing it in his own room, much to my disappointment.

"We need to eat," he replies with a shrug.

"But the team will be there."

"And?"

"Well, they might say something—"

"*And?*"

"I—" I nibble at my bottom lip. "Smitty—"

He tucks me closer. "Smitty doesn't have any room to talk," he says. "Hell, half the guys on the team don't considering they're in the same boat and have all taken their sweet time to get their heads out of their asses about their women."

"I guess."

Slowing, he shifts me so I'm facing him, so our eyes have no choice but to meet. "We're doing this?"

"Wh-what?" I ask, slowing to a halt.

"Us," he says. "Last night, you made it clear you want this. Want more than sex. Want an *us*...along with the rest of it. Well —" A breath, his big chest expanding and compressing, before he adds quietly, "Well, I want it too."

Damn.

He's fucking wonderful.

All he went through, all that's still tearing him apart, and he's letting me in.

So, I don't have to find the courage, find the strength.

I can just...*live*.

Live the life I want and see where it takes me and trust that he won't push me away again.

I exhale, lift my chin, straighten my shoulders and declare, "We're doing this."

He gently touches my cheek. "So Smitty and the guys don't matter. I can handle them," he adds when I start to protest. "And yeah, they're my family too, so I don't mean they don't matter in our lives. I just...they don't get to weigh in on this decision. Us first and then the rest of the world, yeah?"

My heart squeezes and I feel myself fall in love with Jackson, just a little bit, right there and then.

Hell, who am I kidding?

I've been half in love with him for years.

This is just me tipping over the edge, descending the slippery slope, knowing the inevitable outcome.

"You and me versus the world," I agree.

His mouth kicks up. "Damn right, kitty cat."

My cheeks heat. "I don't know if I can handle you calling me that in public. Not now that I know what you mean when you say it"

"You'll get used to it." He leans down, kisses the top of my ear. "Especially when I worship that pussy exactly as it deserves to be worshiped."

Weak knees. My pulse pounding in my veins.

But I don't protest when he wraps his arm around my shoulders and draws me toward the restaurant of the hotel...

And into a head-on collision with the Breakers Gossip Train.

CHAPTER TWENTY-TWO

Jackson

"Yo, asshole!"

I grind my teeth together because I was waiting for this.

Ever since breakfast at the hotel—spent with Claire at my side, feeling more settled, more secure and comfortable than I have in years, even though Smitty was glaring daggers at me —I knew this shit was coming.

I turn, snag the ball of tape out of mid-air before it smacks me in the face. "What?" I grit out, tossing it in the trash and moving to my station. I wish we were done with this road trip, wish I could bring Claire back to my place, spend hours kissing every single inch of her body.

But we have a hockey game and then a late flight home.

We'll all be exhausted—not just us players, but also the support staff, including Luc and Claire.

I might be able to bring her home, or talk my way into her bed, but it's going to be to sleep.

Because no way in hell is her first time going to be a quickie because we're both running on fumes.

"What are you doing?" Smitty booms, dropping into the chair next to mine—another not fun part of being the away team? The shitty locker room digs.

I miss my cold pool and personalized cubby.

Thankfully, I don't miss it enough to be daydreaming about that shit.

Instead, I'm aware and on edge and...

I duck when he throws the punch.

"She's like our little sister," he growls. "How dare you take advantage of her?"

One second, I'm half amused, half annoyed at the pushy asshole routine that Smitty's displaying. The next, the words process, my temper snaps, and I'm on my feet, my hand around his throat.

Squeezing.

Squeezing *very* hard.

Squeezing until his face starts turning red.

"I would never take advantage of her," I hiss, leaning up so that our faces are mere inches apart, so that he can see exactly how deadly serious I am. "I barely got my own head out of my ass enough to accept taking her on a date, let alone that I can have something more. It's her," I say. "It's her and me, and you're not going to do *anything* to fuck that up."

If I was in my right mind, I might have noticed that all of a sudden, Smitty is smirking.

Even though my hand is still around his throat.

Even though I'm still squeezing the life out of him like I'm trying to get that last fucking drop of juice out of a crushed slice of lemon.

But I *don't* notice.

Because I'm too fucking pissed.

"I don't owe you a fucking explanation," I growl. "But I know you care about her, so I'll give you this. I like her— maybe too much and for far too fucking long. I just didn't think I was good enough for her. Lucky for me, she disagrees and has decided to give my dumb ass a chance." I bend, holding his gaze. "So, I'm not going to fuck it up. Not now. Not—"

A hand on my shoulder nearly has me whipping around and punching out whoever in the fuck thinks that they're allowed to touch me right now.

"I get the urge to strangle Smitty," Aiden says quietly, "but kill him and we'll be down a defenseman tonight." His mouth quirks. "I'd really prefer this big asshole block the shots instead of me."

That's just absurd enough to have laughter bubbling up in my chest...

And my hand releasing.

Smitty—who's big enough that he likely could have easily broken my hold—coughs loudly (because he does everything loudly). "You're not ready, dickwad," he says. "You barely function with the rest of the team, barely let us in. How are you going to begin to take care of our Claire properly?"

My biggest fucking fear on display, but instead of making me retreat, I'm ready to dig in and push forward.

She's too important to give up just because I'm scared.

I narrow my eyes at him. "I'm fucking ready."

"No," he growls. "You're not."

I open my mouth to tell him to fuck off but he, in typical Smitty fashion, can't shut the fuck up.

"You'll hurt her and then *I'll* hurt you and—"

"Asshole," I begin, stepping close. "You'd better watch your fucking mouth."

"Smitty," Aiden says on a sigh, moving between us, shoving us back so I'm out of choking reach. Assholes. Both of them. "Enough," he says. "Claire can take care of herself, and Jackson isn't going to hurt her—not on purpose, anyway. Because we're all inherently dumbasses and are going to fuck up, but—" He looks at Smitty when the other man growls.

"But," he says again, "Jackson and Claire have us, have you and each other, and they'll be good, yeah?"

Silence falls—a fucking shock, especially with Smitty around.

"And you," Aiden goes on, turning back to me, eyes colder and expression more serious than I've ever see it. "We haven't missed that you've been a dick to her more than once over the last months. I'm glad you've made your peace and seem to have gotten on board with how great she is, and I hope to fuck you got on your fucking knees and groveled for forgiveness—"

Groveling for forgiveness isn't the worst idea.

Especially considering how big of an asshole I've been.

"But Claire looked happy at breakfast, and I heard about yesterday—"

Of course he had.

Fucking Gossip Train.

"—so I'll just say, keep doing what you're doing. Keep making her smile and spoiling her and making her happy." His eyes cool further. "And so long as you do that, we won't have to kill you."

"Swear to God," Walker says quips, "that's more words at once than I've ever heard you say."

Aiden rolls his eyes, nods toward my equipment, silently telling me to get my shit together and get ready for the game.

"I'm more impressed by the fact that Jackson managed to lift Smitty's heavy ass at least two inches off that chair," Raph chimes in.

"Superhero strength," Cas says. "Only happens in cases of emergencies and extreme rage."

"Or from the drugs," Marcel deadpans.

Now it's my turn to roll my eyes—they heard my mom ask me *one* time about being high (blood sugar high, not high high) and the joke has continued.

It doesn't help that I technically also take drugs multiple times a day.

The locker room laughs in appreciation of our captain's joke, and I exhale, allowing the dredges of anger to fade away as I return Aiden's fist bump with one of my own.

Then I start getting dressed.

And not a moment too soon.

Because Claire walks through the door barely a minute later, carrying our pregame snacks.

Including my sandwich.

I thank her for it with a kiss, with a murmured, "I'll repay you later," that has her blushing, and then I'm focusing on Smitty, glaring at him while he glares at me.

I'll show him.

I'll show them all.

But most of all, I'll show Claire—

How fucking perfect she is.

"You don't have to repay me," she says quietly.

"And you don't have to do what you do." I tuck a strand of hair behind her ear. "But you do it anyway." I lean close. "Plus, I think you have all sorts of interesting *thoughts* about how exactly I can pay you back."

Her cheeks go redder, but she's smiling when she pecks me on the cheek—thus earning a roomful of catcalls. "It's forty-three minutes till game time," she says, shoving my sandwich toward my mouth. "Get busy."

She winks.

"Now *and* later."

I grin.

Then she waves and slips from the room, hurrying off to make magic elsewhere.

My gaze catches on Smitty's and I don't miss that now instead of glaring at me…

He's looking thoughtful.

Which is more than enough progress for today.

Especially—I take a bite of my PB&J—because I plan on making him block all the fucking shots tonight as payback.

CHAPTER TWENTY-THREE

Claire

I was expecting this.

I just was expecting it sooner.

Smitty's waited an entire week between my whirlwind start with Jackson on the road trip and today to find a time to corner me.

The whirlwind has continued, really, and I've had far less time with Jackson than I wanted.

Mostly because we slept that first day away, both of us exhausted by the game that ran long because of a shit-ton of penalties being called—on both teams—and a delayed flight on our return trip home. Then, the next morning, I had to zip over to Gran's because she had a burst pipe.

Her basement was flooded, with sewage no less.

Thankfully, Jackson saved the day, stopping by with a plumber friend and taking Gran and me out to dinner once things were under control.

But the damage was...a lot.

And disgusting.

And so, Gran's staying at my place.

I love it, love that I get this time with her, but between getting her necessary things to my apartment and cooking, cleaning, and setting her up in my guest room, I've barely had time for work.

Something that's made harder with the obscenely busy game and practice schedule this week. It's meant that Luc and I have been running around, and the guys working their asses off, and—

That I haven't had a lot of time to do anything but sleep, soak in what little private time Jackson and I have had (minimal at best), and cram work into any available moment.

Well, anyway, I guess it's not really a surprise that it's taken a week for this conversation to take place.

"I texted you," I say softly.

"Texts hide a lot of shit," he mutters, eyes fixed on mine. "Are you really okay?"

"Frazzled. Busy as hell. Exhausted." I sigh. "But happier than I've ever been. It's like...well, like you said, practice makes perfect, and Jackson and I are working on perfect."

His eyes narrow. "It's been a week."

"And sometimes that week is enough for you to know what's very right and what's very wrong in your life," I tell him.

He scowls, but I see it.

The softening on the edges of his expression.

So, I give him what he needs to be at ease.

"I told you I was tired of being on the sidelines, but terrified to jump onto the field alone, terrified to let anyone in. Jackson"—this time my sigh is contented—"well, he makes me forget I was scared in the first place. I can't say that it's going to be all adorable puppies and rainbows now that we got our shit together, but I'm happy and excited to be out here living."

Silence.

His scowl deepening.

"What?" I ask, genuinely confused.

"I hate that I don't have a chance to punch that smug fucker in the nose."

"Liar," I tease. "You're upset we found our way to each other without you interfering and playing matchmaker."

He waggles his brows. "Who says I didn't?"

"What?"

"A pointed question in the locker room?" he asks archly. "Questioning whether he's capable enough? Coaching you through the scary bits so that you were open to a new opportunity?" He sobers. "The asshole from the first date nearly fucked it all up, but luckily, I knew that Jackson had a white knight hidden beneath all that black armor."

"You couldn't have known all of that."

He blows on his knuckles, buffs them on his shoulder. "Couldn't I?"

"Now I know why Jackson tried to strangle you," I grumble, pushing off the wall, intending to head back to my office.

"You heard about that?"

It's my turn to waggle my brows. "I hear everything. I know all."

A glare. "And you didn't give your man an ass-chewing about hurting me?"

"You're big." I shrug, but I'm biting back a smile. "Plus, I know he didn't really hurt you. For one," I say, "he wouldn't, and you know that as much as I do."

He opens his mouth, but I keep talking.

"For another, both Kailey and Samantha"—his wife and my friend and the team's head trainer, also my friend—"told me that you didn't even have the tiniest bruise."

"I did *too*."

"Did not," I say because I'm a child.

"Did too."

I'm grinning, happier than ever, soul light, heart singing with joy.

Because I'm living, even if it's to get into a silly, joking argument with my friend.

I rise up on tiptoe, press a kiss to his bearded cheek. "Did not."

"Did—"

I drop back onto my heels. "Tell you what."

"What?"

"Next time that Jackson tries to strangle you, I'll make sure you don't get a boo-boo."

His lips twitch. "Rude." A beat. "What about if I decide to strangle *him?*"

"You won't," I say. "Because you don't like hurting people either."

He opens his mouth.

"But you know," I add in a hurry, knowing it *has* to be a hurry, otherwise I won't get my words in over him, "all of this is because you helped me realize how much I'm missing by hiding in the shadows."

"Clairey girl," he rumbles, eyes gentle, voice soft. He reaches out to hug me.

I step back, my eyes stinging, but I ignore them.

Know that's enough sappy for this early in the morning.

Otherwise I'll be full watering pot.

"Plus," I say, so sickeningly sweet that he smiles at me, just for a moment—

At least until the rest of my words process.

"—you know that if you hurt him, I'll hurt *you.*"

Then his eyes widen.

And his mouth drops open.

And...I take advantage of having Smitty on his back foot for once, spinning on my heel, starting for my office and the work that waits for me there.

But I'm barely two feet away before my watch buzzes.

Stomach clenching, I glance down, worried it'll be another crisis with Gran.

Thankfully, though, the message makes me smile.

It *is* from Gran.

But…it's from the Gran of old telling me—

Bingo. Tonight. Get your dabber hand ready.

My heart leaps.

Living. We're all starting to live again—me and Jackson and even, Gran…

Albeit with the aid of a little hockey player magic.

I smile and my phone buzzes again a heartbeat later with a message I know will be from Jackson.

Mission accomplished.

"Smitty?" I ask, turning back, finding him still standing there, gaping at me like I've lost my mind—

Or maybe like I've finally found the courage to live my life.

"Yeah, Clairey girl?" he asks, sounding more than a bit befuddled.

Clairey girl, one.

Smitty bitty, zero. Or maybe a hundred, but—I mentally shrug—I'm not going to admit that.

I'm going to focus solely on battles from today.

Okay, on battles from the last thirty minutes.

Okay, on battles from this hallway in the last ninety seconds.

Winning.

"How do you feel about bingo?"

CHAPTER TWENTY-FOUR

Jackson

"I told you that this is serious business," Claire murmurs as we walk slowly into the auditorium later that night.

Slowly because Gran only moves at one speed.

"I know," I murmur back. "I just didn't…"

I take a look at the packed room, full to the brim of people and tables and noise. The lights are bright as hell and there's a table with an emcee on the far side of the space, along with a huge gaily lit board of numbers. The other side has a huge setup of even more tables, all topped with food.

"…this."

"It's a popular event," Gran says, shuffling forward.

I hang back so I can whisper in Claire's ear. "Is that the infamous cake you mentioned before?"

She smiles, fucking beams with happiness from the inside out.

I know it's because I remember, because it's one of those small things.

But she doesn't get sappy on me—we've got the serious

business of bingo to conquer—just nods and presses a kiss to my cheek. "Don't worry," she says. "I know how to sweet talk my way into a piece of red velvet."

My favorite.

Another small thing.

One that has me taking her hand, lacing our fingers together, and following Gran to what's presumably our table...

Not presumably, I realize.

It's filled with hockey players.

I smother a grin—Claire's magic at work.

Gran doesn't seem surprised, just sidles right in and drops into a chair.

"Come on," Claire says, drawing me to the front of the room. "We need cards before they run out."

"What?" But I follow her as she zips up to the front, pausing in front of an older woman with sleek gray hair and a ready smile.

"I need cards for Gran and me," Claire says, then hitches her thumb over her shoulder. "And for a table full of newbies."

I know that she's teasing, especially with the grin she tosses my way, but I still bristle anyway. I don't like being called a newbie at anything, least of all at something as simple as crossing off some numbers.

"Trust me," she murmurs, batting my hand away when I go to pay, before gathering up sheaves of paper and tubes with colored caps that she's called dabbers.

"I—" I reach for her, intending to help, but I don't get the chance.

She's gone, arms full, but that doesn't stopping her from zigzagging through the crowd and making her way back to the table.

I follow a lot less gracefully, managing to get to the table in time to hear Smitty and Gran going at it—both of them looking like they're having the times of their lives as they bicker.

"Are you ready to get your butt kicked, big guy?" Gran asks, holding up a dabber threateningly.

"I'll remind you that I can crush you like a toothpick, little lady," he replies, snagging the dabber and pretending like he's going to launch it across the room.

"You ruin my lucky dabber," Gran threatens, "and I'll break all of your hockey sticks."

Smitty shrugs. "The team will buy more."

"Umm," I mutter.

"Smitty's met Gran before," Claire tells me with a small smile. "Or they've engaged in verbal shenanigans before."

I look back to the pair, listen to the banter—or threats of dabber abuse—continuing, but not for long because Claire's nudging me into a seat and giving me a Cliff's Notes version of the rules and how to properly use the dabber and what the hell a Four Stamps game is—which is the second game (apparently there's more than one type of bingo and more than one game?) we're playing tonight.

"Wait, wait!" Smitty booms halfway through. "Those two are sharing state secrets over there. No cheating." He narrows his eyes at my woman, earning a glare from me. "Tell me everything you told him."

Claire sighs and shakes her head. "I was just explaining the rules."

He makes a Matrix-style come-on-then hand gesture.

Another sigh, but she gives him the rundown—and I don't miss that the guys snap on their game faces and prepare for battle too.

Raph practices proper dabbing procedure.

Marcel flips through the pages of his bingo card—a misnomer I think because there are six cards on every sheet in the stack.

Smitty focuses, beyond serious as he absorbs every word of Claire's instructions.

Walker gets his space ready, perfectly laying everything out.

And I'm…I'm watching Claire talk and get everyone comfortable, effortlessly knowing what they need without being pushy (though she seems to ride that line a little with her grandmother, something I get, but something I know she struggles to reel in).

"She's great, isn't she?"

I turn to see another older woman, this one with carefully coiffed hair, her mouth curved into a gentle smile. One look and I know instantly who this is.

"June," I say, extending my hand. "I'm Jackson."

"Oh, I know," she replies, shaking my hand with a firm confidence that belies her size.

"How?"

She winks. "Gran"—a nod at the woman, who's holding court amongst the hockey players now that Claire's finished with instructions (aside from Cas who, as always, has several tactical follow up questions)—"gave me the scoop. Tall, dark, and handsome who looks at her granddaughter just right? Easy pickings." A beat. "How did you know I was me amongst all these other senior citizens?"

I grin, flick my gaze down to her sweater, which is covered in corgis—a breed she's apparently obsessed with.

"Damn," she says lightly. "I outed myself, huh?"

"Sorry to say it, but yes."

Someone calls her name, and she sighs. "Duty calls and as much as I'd love to keep chatting, I need to be ready for anything."

"For cake throws and dabber revolts?"

Her mouth curves. "Exactly." She touches my shoulder, leans in. "Keep looking at her right, yeah?"

Then she's gone.

"Oh," I hear from next to me, turning to see that Claire is done talking with Cas.

"What?"

"I wanted to catch up with Junie before she gets too busy." She makes a face as she clocks exactly what I have. "Too late, apparently."

I take her hand, lean in and press a kiss to her temple. "You were wrong."

She frowns. "About what?"

"You say you lived on the sidelines, that you hid your heart and didn't let anyone in, but—" I nod at a table full of hockey players getting ready to battle senior citizens in bingo alongside her grandmother, at the woman who cares enough to remind me to treat her right. "You have all of *this*."

"Grumpy old people and surly hockey players?"

My mouth quirks. Because I know she reads me, hears me...

But also get why she doesn't want heavy right now.

This is the first time Gran's out in ages. I'm here. The guys are locked and loaded.

She wants a good night.

And I know that I was talking a big talk when I allowed myself to get to this point, to have her, to pursue this draw between us—saying that I was going to let her go when she was done with me so I'd make that first move.

But I some part of me also knew...

That was never going to happen.

Letting her go.

Letting her be done with me.

She's mine. I've fallen deep and hard, and I fucking love her.

Which is why I give her the out.

Why I give her what she needs to enjoy the night.

I touch her cheek and deliberately change the subject to light.

"What are the odds that Smitty causes a cake riot?"

CHAPTER TWENTY-FIVE

Claire

Smitty doesn't, in fact, cause a cake riot.

But it's a close thing because he gets bingo twice.

"I don't care if you have an entire blackout," Jackson had growled at him, "but if you win another fucking round and make trouble for Junie"—because our neighbors at a nearby table looked ready to commit dabber-cide—"I will gleefully throw you to the permed, cat-sweater-wearing old ladies."

Smitty had taken a look around and wisely shut his mouth for the duration of the night.

Even though, I'm pretty sure I saw he had a bingo in the last game.

Now, I watch as Jackson carries Gran, passed out and exhausted from all the activity of the evening. I'd feel bad if not for the fact that she had a great night, one of the best in a while, smiling and ordering the guys around, grumbling when her numbers weren't pulled, eating not one but two giant slices of cake.

She hadn't seemed tired.

But the moment we hit the highway, she was *out*.

Snoring away in the back seat, leaving Jackson and I to share quiet looks as he navigated back to my place.

Now, he settles her on the bed and leaves me to get her comfy and tuck her into bed. She doesn't move as I take off her shoes, set her glasses on the side table, along with her purse, and plug in her phone, doesn't so much as make a peep as I turn off the lights and step out into the hall.

And find it empty.

Frowning, I move down the hall toward the sliver of light shining onto the carpet and push into the bedroom.

And freeze, heart squeezing.

Jackson has a pair of my pajamas in his hands. "You should get some sleep, kitty cat," he murmurs, holding them out to me. "You've had a long week."

He's right.

We're both tired, and it's been an exhausting series of days.

But…it's also the first time we've been alone together and upright and—

I move to him, take the pajamas from his hand, and drop them to the foot of the bed. And then…I wrap my arms around him.

"Sweetheart?"

I kiss him, put all of that practice makes perfect of the last week to good use.

He responds in a flash of movement, groan rumbling through his chest, arms banding around my middle, tongue thrusting into my mouth, kissing me until my lungs protest, and only then does he release my mouth. He reaches for the hem of my sweater, yanking it up and over my head, tossing it to the side, allowing me to do the same to his tee, to get up close and personal with his hard chest and muscular abs and—

I freeze for a second, not knowing where to go, what to do with all of this.

Kiss or lick, touch or bite.

I want to do it all and I want to do it all right now and—

"Oh!" I gasp when he wraps his fingers around my wrist and tugs, sending us both toppling to the mattress.

I land on top of him with a rush of air but don't get to catch my breath because he's kissing me again. "Don't feel over-whelmed, kitty cat. We stop at any time, remember?"

Sweet man.

My man.

"I love you," I whisper.

His eyes go wide, but this time, I kiss him.

"And I'm not overwhelmed," I say when I manage to tear my mouth away from his. "Or not in the way you think," I tell him when he begins to protest. "There are so many things I want to do to you, and I don't know where to start," I admit. "Kiss your chest, suck at your nipples, reach my hand into your pants and stroke your…" I swallow because I may be a virgin, but I'm not an idiot. I read romance novels. I'm a pro with my vibrator. But something about giving voice to all of this is…

Vulnerable.

But only for a second because then he's flipped us, my back pressing into the mattress, his big body boxing me in. "First," he whispers. "I love you too."

My lungs inflate in a rush.

"I think that's why I fought it so much." His mouth curves. "I knew that if I gave in, I'd never have any hope of keeping you out, and after you discovered what I did"—he touches my cheek—"it was easier to be mad and push you away than delve into it."

"You're a good person."

He exhales. "I think I am, but—" A shake of his head. "I'm still working on really accepting that."

I want him to believe it down to the very marrow of his bones.

But…

Practice makes perfect.

One step at a time.

"And second," he says, heat slipping back into his eyes, his mouth near enough that when he speaks, the words brush against my lips, dance down my tongue, "I want you to stroke my cock and kiss any part of me you want, but we have time," he murmurs. "*So* much time for this."

"I have years to make up for," I counter.

His mouth twitches up at the corners. "That's true enough, kitty cat. So, how about for tonight you just tell me one of those fantasies?"

So many.

There have been *so* many.

But one stands out.

And…

I don't hesitate to tell him.

And…

He doesn't hesitate to make it come true for me.

Slowly dispensing of both of our clothes, kissing me until my breaths come in rapid, short gusts, until my lips tingle and feel swollen. Then moving down to my breasts, sucking at my nipples, sending my nerves alight with sensation, leaving me needy and wet and…

Ready for his mouth when he crawls down my body and licks me between my legs, slowly, like we really do have all the time in the world. Focusing on my clit and using the flat of his tongue to drive me crazy as he fucks me with a finger, in and out, in and out, steady and smooth and unhurried.

I gasp as he slips a second and then a third finger in, knowing he'll be bigger, that I'll need the preparation.

And even though, I'm shaking, I'm ready—beyond ready, really—for him. Even though I'm expecting him to draw back after a few minutes, to push inside me and rock us both to completion, he doesn't.

He's still taking his time, not in any rush, and—

"Oh!" I gasp as the orgasm sneakily rolls over me, a wave of sensation that takes me under when I least suspect it.

And still, he's slow and deliberate, coaxing me through the highest peak of sensation, deliberate as he touches me and draws out my pleasure.

I'm limp when I hear the distant crinkle of a condom wrapper opening, but I manage to peel one eye open.

"We can stop here," he murmurs, noticing that I'm watching him—because of course he does.

"I want it all," I tell him, reaching for his arms and drawing him back over me. "With you, I want it all."

"This may hurt." A soft apology as he settles between my legs, thumb coming back to my clit, cock notching at my entrance.

"I'm ready."

He inhales—

And then he's pushing inside, my pleasure easing the way, his thumb making me forget about the burn and stretch. I thank God for my vibrators when he pauses, leaving me feeling as though I'm filled to bursting. They prepared me for this—

Not nearly enough, of course.

But the burn of him inside me is a perfect mix of pleasure and pain.

"Okay?" he rasps.

He's shaking, sweat on his forehead, a wild sort of energy in his body.

But he's holding on, he's waiting.

Making sure I'm okay.

"Perfect," I say, wrapping my leg around his waist, arching my hips to allow him even deeper. "Now," I order. "Give me the rest of it."

And just like always...

He does.

CHAPTER TWENTY-SIX

Jackson

My dick hasn't had nearly enough of her, the taste from last night fucking incredible, fucking perfect—

But not nearly enough.

I managed to get her to come, to feel the clamp of her pussy around my cock before I lost all vestiges of control and came in pathetically few strokes. And I had her again this morning, a quick and furious fuck that ended up with her on top of me, those gorgeous tits bouncing in my face and an orgasm burning down my spine.

But I need more.

I want more.

I need—

"Head's up!"

To keep my fucking head up, I realize, dodging around Raph after nearly plowing into my teammate who's innocently warming up.

"Dude," he mutters.

"Sorry." I don't make an excuse, because I don't have one.

Raph narrows his eyes at me. "Women, man," he mutters before skating off, not giving me shit, because he has a woman who put him through his own ringer—until they stumbled into something that I used to envy.

Now I just…

Want to get there.

Am *going* to get there—Claire and I versus the world.

Claire and I versus the bullshit of our past.

I could hurt—

I cut that thought off as I keep moving across the ice. I could hurt her. I likely will because I can be a complete asshole sometimes, but…I'm going to do what I did with hockey—keep focused on the small details, keep doing better, keep moving forward.

Thinking that would have sent me spiraling even a week ago.

Not today.

Not again.

Because I want Claire.

Because I don't want to fuck it up—

"Dude!"

I blink, realize I nearly mowed Raph over again.

"Sorry," I mutter.

"Maybe go take a walk to the locker room and back, clear your head somewhere you're not going to murder me," he mutters.

Since that's a good idea, I just accept the glare he tosses my way and skate to the bench, keeping my head on a swivel so I don't crush or get crushed by one of my teammates. I stop in the open door.

Taking a couple of deep breaths, I stretch and bide my time, struggling to find my focus. Eventually, I pause in front of the list of drills taped to the panel of the glass just to the right of the door that leads down to the locker room.

And that purpose settles over me, the concentration is suddenly easier to coax to the surface, to hold on to.

A lot of hockey nowadays is enriched by tech, but hell if I don't love a piece of paper listing out our drills.

It feels familiar, like home, like those long days on the rink when I was a kid, like practices with my buddies and games we didn't always win, and my parents cheering for me from the stands.

"Dude," Aiden mutters as he skates by me, shaking his head.

I frown for a second, knowing I didn't almost take *him* out —I'm not blocking the door, and he just emerged out of the hall that leads to the locker room. But when I meet his eyes, he merely juts his chin over my shoulder and I turn and see Smitty lounging against the glass, having apparently employed ninja skills to sneak up behind me.

Either that or I still have my head in the clouds.

Po-tay-to. Po-tah-to.

That—and Smitty's sneaky ninja skills—are the least of my worries because he's standing there, grinning like an idiot and holding a tiny trophy.

I immediately roll my eyes.

Smitty shenanigans never cease.

He holds it up so I can read the inscription—

Bingo Champion of the World.

"What'd you do?" I ask dryly. "Go out first thing this morning and get it?"

"And can you really be a champion of a game of luck?" Aiden asks.

"No, I didn't," he says, holding it carefully against his chest. One big shoulder lifts then drops. "And"—he glances at Aiden—"Claire seems to think so," he says proudly, blowing on the trophy and buffing it on his jersey, "considering she gave it to me this morning."

That's what she was rushing out the door before practice for.

I figured it was a meeting with Luc—and not something to do with the sheet-scorching sex we had last night—because I woke up this morning to her lush little mouth trailing over my chest, on the way to giving me a blowjob.

A blowjob that didn't happen because we both got distracted by the way our bodies felt brushing against each other and then our hands were involved and I couldn't get enough of her mouth, her breasts, that slick little pussy—

Pretty soon I was rolling on a condom, gently stroking home, and then having what I already knew reinforced—Claire is a quick learner. A hand pushed me over to my back, clambered on top of me, and…

She'd rode us both home.

Smitty settles the trophy on the ledge behind the bench then grins as he looks back at me.

"What?" I ask.

"I said you weren't ready."

My stomach knots.

"I was wrong."

"What?" I ask, going for light, knowing he doesn't buy that shit in the least. "Connor Smith admitting that he's wrong? I don't believe it. I'd better write this day down in history."

His brows drag together, but he doesn't fuck around—then again, he never does.

"You've been through the shit, man," he says. "And I don't mean with the bullshit your body pulled with your pancreas—"

I inhale, find that I'm holding myself very still.

"I mean all of it—" His gaze hits mine, holds and…

I know.

That he knows.

That he's *known*.

And Claire was right—not once has he treated me like I used to think I deserved.

Not once has he looked at me like I thought I should be viewed.

Fuck, my woman is smart.

"I need to go," I mutter.

He catches my shoulder when I hop onto the bench, intending to haul ass down to—

"Easy, man," he says, grip unbreakable. "I've never—"

I turn, my eyes hitting his. "I know." I cover his hand with my own, squeeze and peel it free. "I know. Finally, I fucking *know*. And"—I shake my head—"she knew without even knowing."

Smitty's expression is almost gentle. "Of course she did," he tells me. "She's smart as fuck and pays attention."

"To all the things, both big and small." I tilt my head toward the hall. "And I need to go tell her how right she is."

"About the big shit?" he asks.

"About *everything*."

Smitty grins and claps me on the shoulder so hard I swear I feel like the brackets on my skates are going to give way—either that or I'm going to be shoved straight through the ice down to the concrete below.

"Now you've fucking got it."

He nudges me off the ice.

"Now you fucking know."

I do.

I fucking know.

And I'm not going to let anything stop me.

CHAPTER TWENTY-SEVEN

Claire

There's a perfunctory knock at my office door that has my fingers freezing above the keyboard.

I look up to see the wooden panel swing inward in a rush and my stomach clenches.

I lurch to my feet, chair skidding backward, colliding with the wall, then start to hurry around my desk. "Oh my God, Jackson, is everything—"

My words stopper up in my throat.

Then escape in an indiscernible squeak as he rushes forward and scoops me up.

His eyes are wild, his color is high, and—

All of a sudden, he's kissing me.

Deep and wet with lots and lots of tongue, stealing my breath with his lips, with the tight hold of his arms, with the way he swings me up and pins me against the door.

Even then, he doesn't stop kissing me, not until I grip the hair at the base of his neck, knocking his helmet to my office floor, dragging his mouth away from mine. "Need…" I pant. "To… Breathe."

"Meh," he says, chest heaving. "Air is overrated."

And then he's kissing me again, his hand moving between us to lift up my skirt.

I shiver. "Don't you have practice?"

"Don't fucking care," he mutters, having bunched my skirt to mid-thigh, his fingers moving to the waistband of my underwear and dragging them down. "Need you. Need you right fucking now."

This is a fantasy I haven't had—Jackson frantic with need, fucking me up against my office door. My poor innocent brain would have never been able to conjure this scenario up before, would have never begun to dream that a man could want me like this.

Thank fuck I've been disabused of that notion.

Thank fuck I have a whole lot of inspiration for new fantasies involving this man.

Office sex.

Skirt hiking.

Jackson showing exactly how far gone he is when he shoves down his hockey pants and positions his dick at my center.

I have just the thread of consciousness left to say, "Condom."

He freezes then groans and drops his head against my shoulder. "I don't have my wallet."

"But I have my purse," I say, reaching hard to the right, straining when I feel the thin leather strap. I tug the small bag from the coat rack, unzip it quickly, and then extract the condom I've kept there ever since Gran taught me about safe sex. "Not expired," I say. "I change it out every six months because…" I feel my cheeks heat. "Because I didn't—"

He presses his lips to mine for one brief, scorching hit. "I'm

caveman enough to be glad to have you all for myself."
Another kiss. "And even more glad that you have *this*."

He rolls the condom down the length of his cock and even
though I'm getting door sex, even though I'm getting him like
this, in his gear in my office in the middle of the day, the risk of
being caught or at least gossiped about high, even though it's
new and exciting and a little terrifying, I know he'll make it good.

Just like I know my mind won't stop coming up with new
fantasies.

That I intend to act out, whether it's in the bedroom *or* my
office.

"Ready?" he asks, lifting me a little higher, notching the
head of his cock at my entrance.

"For you?" I say, pressing my palm to his cheek. "Forever
and always."

His eyes close for a brief second, the emotion in the deep
brown depths calling to my heart, my soul. "Fuck, I love you."

"I—" But my words are cut off by another squeak as he
thrusts home.

I'm sore, yes. He's big and this is a lot for my poor virginal
pussy.

But I don't tell him to stop, don't *want* him to stop.

It's glorious when he pushes deep, sending my ass
smacking against the door, and just as glorious when he draws
back until just the tip of his cock is inside me. "More?"

"Yes." I nip at his bottom lip. "Now."

His smirk may be the sexiest thing I've ever seen.

But I don't get to do more than commit that to memory
before he's listening to my orders, slamming into me, pulling
out, thrusting again and again and *again*.

Until I feel that heat gathering in my belly.

Until my nerves are tingling with sensation.

Until my vision hazes and my head falls back and my nails
dig into his shoulders and—

Until I come apart.

"Oh, my God," I whisper. "Oh, my—"

And then there are no more words.

Just pleasure that threatens to tear me apart. And a man who helps keep me together.

"Christ," he growls when his own orgasm yanks him under, his thrusts going choppy and uneven, my name tumbling off his lips. "You feel." A thrust. "So fucking." Another. "Good."

It's long moments later before I'm able to speak, to hold myself up when he settles my feet carefully on the ground.

His hands rest on either side of my face. "I love you."

I inhale, open my mouth—

"And you were right."

I exhale. "About what?"

"Smitty knows."

More breath, though this time it's sharp and deep and nearly has me choking out, "H-he does?"

"He does, and he's known for a long time, I think and—" He shoves a hand through hair. "He's never treated me differently. I mean, I was starting to get there"—he drops his hand—"because of you."

My throat is tight.

"But some part of me thought..." He sighs and shakes his head.

"That it still might find a way to come back and hurt you."

"Yeah."

I take his hand. "Smitty knows."

He exhales. "Which means that Luc probably knows."

I nod.

"*You* know."

Another incline of my head.

"And you love me."

"I do."

"And so do my parents."

"Yes."

He closes his eyes, drops his chin to his chest. "I wasted a fuck-ton of time. You could have been mine long ago."

"I'm yours now."

He lifts his head, mouth curving. "You and me versus the world?"

"Yes." I grin, drop my hands to his chest. "Along with you and me practicing until we get to perfect," I say lightly. "Because I have lots and *lots* of ideas."

His smile is wolfish, and he opens his mouth—

Knock. Knock. *Knock!*

Jackson groans.

Then again when Smitty's voice echoes through the door.

"Come on, Boxie!" he calls. "We have hockey to play!"

CHAPTER TWENTY-EIGHT

Jackson

"Ready?" Aiden asks, eyes locking with mine, and we've played together long enough that I know exactly what that look means, know exactly where to move when the puck drops and he wins the draw back to Smitty at the point.

I fake like I'm cutting to the middle, prepping for the tip while Marcel sweeps in along the side, stopping their forwards from taking away Smitty's space for the shot.

And just like planned, their D follow me to the net…

And then away from it, freeing up space in front, giving Smitty the chance…

To fake a shot and pass it over to his defensive partner…

Who's streaking in, using his speed to blow by the assholes standing flat-footed on the other team, bracing for a rocket of a shot that doesn't come.

It's a second at most—that we catch them off-guard. We're all athletes, trained and coached to respond to the rapid-fire speed of the game, the second-to-second changes that mean we always have to be thinking three steps ahead.

But we have them for that second.

And it's enough.

I grit my teeth and move back to the net, my defensive tail following me and giving me a love tap—aka a crosscheck to my spine that sends my teeth rattling—for my trouble. I brace myself, take my position, track my team, the puck, the possible permutations…and I hold my ground.

Chaos.

We're down a goal and we *need* chaos, need traffic in front of the net, asses in faces, anything to obscure the goalie's view of the puck and the shot that's going to be coming his way.

Crack!

Right now.

Coming the goalie's way right now.

I try to get out of the way, but I don't fully succeed. I feel the impact of the puck against my foot, the pain radiating up my ankle, my leg.

That'll leave a fucking bruise.

But I'm already spinning, trying to anticipate the deflection, trying to get to a spot where the puck has gone.

There!

I lurch for it, my stick and feet tangling with a guy from their team who sees the puck at the same time I do.

We collide, a jarring moment of impact that threatens to take me out of the play.

But I don't allow myself to stop, to fall, to *lose* this battle.

I push, getting the tip of my stick on the puck, flicking it forward…

Guiding it over…

The goalie scrambles, shooting his leg across the crease, and I know I'm out of time.

I dive, manage to give that puck just another push, light as fuck, but I do it as I'm shoved to the ice amongst a chaotic cluster of sticks and skates…

And it's enough.

I propel it over the line, sending it flying into the back of the net.

Silence—but only for one brief moment.

Because then the home crowd explodes—their cheers rocketing through the arena, loud enough to make my ears hurt.

But as Aiden helps me up to my feet and we skate to the bench, all of that electric energy from the fans, from executing a play we've been working on perfecting for months, I'm aware of only one thing.

One person.

She's standing in the hall today, watching me with a huge grin on her face.

I grin back.

"I knew you could do it," she mouths.

That hits me, deep and perfectly painful, an exquisite sort of pleasure that has me wanting to find her office all over again, to watch her face as I tell her how much she means to me, as I feel her come apart in my arms.

But I have a game to play.

And she has a job to do.

And...I'm not going to let her down.

Not ever again.

———

Her surprise hits me after the game, and I feel it the moment I walk into the bare bones office she keeps at the arena.

Her tricked-out space is at the practice facility, where we spend the bulk of our prep time, both on and off the ice. This room is function over all else, and because there are no distractions, I immediately sense it.

Her tension. Her shock.

Her sadness.

"Shit, kitty cat," I say, shutting the door behind me. "What's the matter?"

She jumps, nearly upending the papers in her hands, then nibbles at her bottom lip, expression unfathomable.

"Is it Gran?" I ask, gut immediately churning.

That snaps her out of the haze, and she quickly shakes her head. "No, honey. I—" Her throat bobs. "It's—"

But she doesn't say anything for a long moment.

And my worry grows.

"I don't think I can tell you," she whispers.

I frown. "What do we say? It's you and me—"

"Versus the world," she finishes. "But this isn't about me. Or you," she adds when that churning in my gut intensifies.

"Who?" I ask.

"I can't say," she whispers. "Not until he knows."

The pieces slide into place then, and they do nothing to ease the anxiety tearing through my insides.

It's nearing the trade deadline.

Players are being shifted around left and right and—

Tears contained in her beautiful eyes, turning those dark brown eyes into liquid pools of chocolate. The tension in her frame, her jaw, like she's expecting me to push.

"I didn't make the deal," she says, her words coming fast and furiously, almost with indiscernible speed, all jumbled together in a rush. "Luc and well, I wasn't part of it, probably because he knows I wouldn't be able to handle it and—" Her voice breaks. "He'd be right. This fucking sucks and I need to be there when we tell him. But how the *hell* am I going to be there?"

"Kitty cat." I shove a hand through my hair, debating on the right thing to say.

Then I decide there's no right thing to say, so I just cross to her, take her in my arms, and I hug her tight.

She sniffs. "It's the job," she whispers. "I know that. I just—"

"We're family," I finish for her when she doesn't say anything further, just wraps her arms around me and continues to breathe, albeit shakily. "It'll be okay," I promise.

Because I'll make sure of that.

And I'd like to say that's why I do what I do next.

But that'd be a lie.

Because, quite simply, I snoop.

I shouldn't. I know I shouldn't, but the way I'm hugging her means that I'm facing her desk.

And the papers are right there and…

It's impossible to not see the name.

Nearly impossible to keep still when I read it.

Nearly impossible to keep holding her, to not let the blow of the trade deal hit me hard enough to reveal that I know.

Easy. *Steady*.

She needs me with her, not worrying about my own emotions.

But…

Aiden. *God*, we've just begun to really gel, and he's becoming a huge part of the team—

And he's my linemate, my teammate, my friend.

How am I going to play without him?

I close my eyes, grab tight to that steady, and keep holding Claire when I'm on more even ground.

Except…

My eyes keep moving over the stack of papers, my brain absorbing the words below—the *name* below.

And this blow is harder.

Because I realize it's not a one-man trade, a simple roster swap for swap.

It's bigger. It's taking two players from our team and bringing four new guys to the Breakers.

Aiden is a tough loss, the worst kind of trade from a player's perspective. He's solid—a great teammate with skills that are still evolving.

But the second subtraction from our roster might just be a death knell our teams.

Because that other Breakers' name on the paperwork?

It's Connor Smith.

CHAPTER TWENTY-NINE

Claire

"...and folks we'll certainly miss our big D-man, Connor Smith," Eva Moreno, the team's broadcaster, says and the sadness in her voice makes it all the harder.

This is the reality of professional sports.

People get traded, rosters are shifted around.

But...Smitty.

And Aiden.

And—

I sniff and turn down the volume of the TV mounted in the corner of my office. I can't watch this any longer, can't hear it. I—

"Claire."

I jerk, gaze going to my open doorway.

"Follow me," Luc mutters.

I look up, stare into my boss's unfathomable expression for a heartbeat, then turn and hurry after him, trying to ignore the somber mood filling the hallways, the far too quiet locker room and training areas.

Smitty.

Christ, even his name trailing through my mind is like a jab to my senses.

"Everything okay?" I ask, trying to remain professional, trying to not think about the fact that a chunk of my heart, my *family* is now traveling two thousand miles to play for the Grizzlies in California. Trying to ignore the fact that I was as blindsided as the rest of the team. I know Luc kept me out of the trade negotiations until they were finalized because he was trying to protect me.

I'm in the depths.

I'm close to the guys—I *have* to be because we work so closely together.

Unfortunately, that means I was just as shocked as the rest of the team.

Luc just grunts in response to my question, so I follow my boss into his office and brace for whatever might be coming my way. The last twenty-four hours have been a whirlwind— trading big players and promising young players, bringing in new prospects and a big-name goalie. I know the moves are necessary to keep building for the future, especially as the guys age out of the game. And I know that Smitty is on the leeward side of his contract, slowly moving to retirement...

But...

Smitty.

And Aiden, I remind myself. I can't discount him. Yeah, Smitty is my big brother, for all intents and purposes, but Aiden is a blow too, a nice guy who's matured into a great man.

Jackson was my rock last night, not pushing me to discuss shit I couldn't. Not upset that I needed to keep it close to my chest.

Just...holding me, bringing me home after the game, running interference between Gran and I so I didn't have to answer tough questions, then tucking me into bed.

I start to sink into the chair in front of Luc's desk, but a flash of movement has my gaze whipping to the right, and I feel tears well up in my eyes when I see Smitty and Aiden standing there.

A squeeze to my shoulder makes me jerk and I stare up into Luc's eyes.

And I see the sadness.

He knows this shit is part of the job, but he hates it as much as I do.

For a moment, we're in perfect harmony, easy to slip into because of all our years together. He's silently telling me that I can do this, that we'll make it through together, that I'm stronger than I think, and more capable too.

My first champion from the Breakers, I realize.

Just…a quiet one.

And he's given me this.

"Office is free all day," he murmurs, and I feel my heart squeeze, but before I can thank him, he's nodding to the guys and slipping out of the room, closing the door softly behind him.

"Claire bear," Smitty says, more subdued than I've ever seen him.

Shit, my throat is suddenly tight and clogged with tears. I try to clear it, try to come up with something meaningful to say, but all I manage is to sniff while forcing out a croaky, "Sm- Smitty.'

He curses softly then opens his big arms and then I'm rushing into them, being embraced by the big, bearded teddy bear. He gives great hugs—because of course he does—but there's something different about the one today.

Because he's hurting too.

Because his life was here and now it's—

"I didn't know," I say in a rush. "Not until Luc told me last night. I didn't— I couldn't have—"

He tugs at my ponytail. "I know Clairey Girl." He drops his

arms and steps back. "But even if you did, I wouldn't have been mad. We"—he hitches his head in Aiden's direction—"both understand that it's the job, that it's out of your control, that this shit is reality."

"Kailey—" His wife had roots her, a life here.

"She's happy, actually," Smitty says. "Happy to be closer to some online friends finally. And sad for all we're leaving behind. And—" His voice is gentle. "*Okay*. Because she knows we'll both be okay. Plus"—he gives Aiden a noogie—"I get to keep torturing the rookie."

"I'm not a rookie anymore," Aiden says on a sigh, making both Smitty and I smile.

Because, in some ways, he'll *always* be a rookie.

"And my family's in California," Aiden says. "I love the guys, but my parents are getting older. It'll be good to be home."

More sharp edges of the pain inside me being filed down, dulled.

Because, of course, Luc would do this as carefully as he could.

Because, of course, we'll all be okay.

"I'm going to miss you knuckleheads," I say, managing to tamp down my tears and not go full watering pot. The emotions are here, boiling just beneath the surface, not going away anytime soon.

But...we'll be okay.

Aiden's cell rings and he glances at the screen, mouth twitching. "My parents." He steps close and pulls me into a hug. "Thank you for everything, Claire Bear. I know we'll see each other soon."

We hug then he slips out into the hall.

Leaving me with the giant teddy bear who made sure I never felt left out.

"Who's going to bring you your pregame snacks or your

favorite drinks or bug you to buy me another Moscow mule at CeCe's?" I whisper.

He hugs me tightly again. "Lucky you have another poor schmuck wrapped around your pinky finger now."

"Thanks to you," I say. "I wouldn't be here without you."

"Damn right, you wouldn't." His lips twitch, a bit of ego clinging to his words. But I know it's all bravado.

Because that's what I'm clinging to as well.

"Meh," I tease. "You know it's just because you're nosy. Jackson and I figured it out by ourselves."

Laughter. A tug at my ponytail. "Rude," he says lightly. "Cutting me out of the fun part."

"I expect a full-blown hockey matchmaking service to be set up in California by the time I visit."

A tap to his bottom lip. "Now, that's not a bad idea at all."

We smile at each other.

Then Smitty's phone beeps.

"I have a plane to catch," he says softly.

"I know."

They have to fly out and meet the Grizzlies on their road trip.

He kisses my cheek, gives me one more beautiful Smitty hug. "I'll see you soon," he promises.

"No chance at getting rid of me," I say, the words watery.

"Damn right."

One more hug.

And then he's gone, slipping out the office door, and disappearing from sight.

From my day-to-day life.

Only *then* do I lose my battle with my tears.

And somehow, it's no surprise that the door opens again and Jackson walks through.

"Luc had me on standby," he whispers as he takes me in his arms. "Let it out, kitty cat."

CHAPTER THIRTY

Jackson

A week later, I roll over and find the mattress next to me empty.

Again.

Claire is functioning much like her old self. She's just...not sleeping.

"Shit," I mutter, sliding out from beneath the blankets and padding to the door. I'll orgasm her ass into oblivion, pin her to the mattress beside me, if I have to, but these half-nights of sleep have got to end.

She needs rest.

She needs to stop beating herself up.

She needs—

I throw on the brakes when I nearly plow into Gran, who's standing outside our bedroom door in a house robe and slippers, her hair in legit curlers.

Fucking cute, like the granddaughter she raised.

The granddaughter she's clearly as worried about as I am.

"You got her?" she asks when I nod in greeting and start for the light shining in the front room of Claire's apartment. We've been alternating nights when the team is in town—one here to keep an eye on Gran, one at my place—but it doesn't matter where we lay our heads.

Claire's still not sleeping through the night.

"I have her," I say. "You on backup duty?"

Her mouth twitches. "I think you'll be fine." A squeeze to my arm. "Just keep pushing at those walls, and she'll eventually get out of her own head enough to talk to you."

I nod and make sure she makes it back into her bedroom safely. We have a big day tomorrow and though she's moving around well from what I've seen—the best in years, according to Claire—there's a frailty that makes me nervous, especially now that she'll be moving back to her place, the flood repair on her basement complete.

Maybe I can convince her and Claire both to move into my house.

Keep them under my watchful eye.

Make sure my woman sleeps and Gran's safe. Make sure there are sunflowers on the counter and the creamer Gran likes is always stocked in my fridge and that she has someone to keep her company.

The plan is already forming in my head as I move out of the hall.

I may not convince either of them anytime soon, but God knows I've learned that putting in the effort is always worth it —especially with these women.

But that's the long game.

The short term priority is coaxing Claire, who's sitting next to the dark window, staring up at the starlit sky, a steaming cup of tea in her hand.

I carefully slip it from her grasp and set it on the table in front of her.

"Sweetheart," I murmur. "You should be sleeping."

"I can't."

"Come on." I put my hand out. "Let's try."

She shakes her head, picks up her tea, avoiding my eyes and whispering into the mug. "How'd Luc know to have you on standby?"

Oh shit.

"Wh-what?"

She looks up and I don't miss the accusation in her eyes. My stomach clenches. "The other day in his office, when I was saying goodbye to the guys, how did Luc know I'd need you?"

I...*fuck.*

Because I snooped and knew what was going on and went right the fuck around my woman to her boss to make sure she had what she needed—the chance to say goodbye and me nearby to pick up the pieces.

"Well, you know the Gossip Train," I prevaricate.

The flash of pain in her eyes—because the captain of the Gossip Train is, *was*, Smitty—ripples through me, stomping all over my insides.

Reminding her of shit I'm trying to take her mind off.

Looking at things I shouldn't.

Doing shit I shouldn't.

Christ.

"No," she says softly. "He didn't know we were together until that morning. He was too busy with the trade deal to pick up that things between us changed." She fixes me in place with a piercing stare. "He told me today."

Damn.

"Kitty cat."

"No," she whispers. "It's you and me versus the world, remember?"

I remember.

It's why I so grossly overstepped.

"I knew something was wrong," I say. "And I know I shouldn't have done it, am fully aware of the irony of me being pissed at you for overstepping when I did the same."

I pause, searching for anything in her face that may reveal what she's feeling.

I can't read shit as she asks, "*How* did you know?"

I cave like a cheap suitcase. "I saw the papers on your desk and snooped."

The barest flicker in her eyes. "When?"

Damn. This makes me sound like even bigger of an asshole.

"When?" she asks a little more firmly.

"When you were crying," I admit. "I saw the papers, saw Aiden's name, and I should have stopped reading. I just... didn't. I have no excuse. I know it was a violation, but when I saw Smitty's name on there, I knew what was tearing you apart." I cup her cheek. "I couldn't force you to talk. I wouldn't do that to you. But...I needed you to be okay, and I know that part of you being okay was that...you needed to say goodbye and then you needed me there to lean on."

"Months ago," she whispers, "I would have revolted at the thought of needing anyone else." Her mouth twitches up. "But Smitty wore me down, made me realize how big and wonderful the world is if I just let it in."

Her eyes are glassy and I wipe away a tear clinging to her lashes. "It is." I kiss her forehead. "And it's kind of funny that he taught me that same lesson."

She sniffs.

I draw her close, hold her for long minutes.

"I should be mad at you for violating my privacy, for going to Luc and making me look weak—"

"He'd do the same for Lex—"

"Maybe," she says. A small smile. "Okay, *certainly*." A beat. "I should be mad at you for interfering, but..." She sighs and her tone grows light, teasing. "I would have done the same thing—*have* done—the same thing."

"True," I agree carefully.

She exhales, mouth curved, eyes gentle. "Thank you for caring enough to do that." A breath. "Thank you for the time to say goodbye." Another. "And thank you for being there afterward."

Relief pours through me, and I draw her close. "Anything for you."

She burrows into my chest. "I love you."

"I want you and Gran to move in with me."

Silence—long enough that I start to panic, especially when she draws back.

But all she does is shrug. "Okay." My mouth falls open and she laughs softly, running her fingers along my jaw. "Gran might be a hard sell," she says, coming close again and pressing a kiss to my cheek, "but I'm down." She leans back and picks up her mug. "Especially because I have no doubt we'll convince her."

Because...

Claire and I versus the world.

"Damn right, we will."

She rests her head against my shoulder then yawns.

Right then.

I draw her into my side, turn us toward the hall. "It's sleep time, kitty cat."

"No," she says softly, footsteps slowing.

I glance down at her, heart—and other things—swelling when I see the mischief in her eyes. "No?" I ask silkily.

"No," she says again, her lips curving. "No sleep."

I lift my brows.

"Because life's too short for sleep when you're living a fantasy," she says.

"Christ, I love you."

A grin but she just leans in, "And speaking of fantasies..."

She lifts on tiptoe, whispers words in my ear that has desire scorching through my insides.

But it's my heart that's on full display when we head off to bed.

When we do everything but sleep.

And I wouldn't have it any other way.

EPILOGUE

Claire, Six Months Later

"I really don't like this," I mutter to Jackson, who's kneeling at my feet, tying up—heaven freaking help me—skates.

"Oh honey," his mom, Kelly, says, patting my arm. "You'll be fine. Jackson is a great teacher."

I smile at her, but don't give voice to the worries tumbling around in my head—

That I've had great teachers before.

That I still nearly brained myself on the ice.

I'm wearing a helmet. And knee pads. And elbow pads. And wrist guards.

Maybe I really *will* be fine.

Especially considering how tightly Jackson is lacing up my skates.

He'll be right there.

Except that I already see the kids from his charity hovering at the edges, wanting face time with him, needing the connection—to a kid who's like them, who has a disease or made mistakes and who's doing something great.

Like connecting people—kids with mentors, kids who feel different or left out or alone in the world with their peers.

He's amazing.

And so is living with him, being in a relationship with him, *loving* him.

Which means, that I need to learn how to skate, or at least cling to the boards well enough so that he can be present and not worried about me and—

He takes my hands and hauls me up to my feet. I waver, but stay upright, likely because he's holding me...and because the skates are so tight.

"See?" he says, guiding me to the door that leads out onto the ice. "You're doing great already."

"You got this!" his mom calls.

I keep my smile in place, but I'm not nearly as confident as Jackson and his mom.

"Bend your knees," his dad, Glen, says. "Use those knee pads to break your fall instead of your butt."

Like falling is a given.

At least the man has read the room.

"Thanks," I whisper.

He leans close. "One lap around the ice and I'll spring you for hot chocolate."

Because even though he has a son who plays professional hockey, he's not a fan of being on the ice.

"Dad," Jackson sighs.

"Double thanks," I say, lifting a fist for him to bump.

"Kitty cat," Jackson says on an equally exasperated breath.

I smile up at him. "Unless I can skip the lap and just go straight to hot cocoa?"

His eyes narrow, but only for a moment, because then a thread of mischief creeps into his eyes as he glances over my shoulder. "What?"

"Someone's come to spring you from skating purgatory." A beat. "At least for a few minutes."

Frowning, I turn and see—

My heart leaps.

"Smitty!" I cry, jumping into his arms, getting that taste of Smitty hug perfection I haven't had in months, not since the Breakers and Grizzlies met just before the playoffs—

With the Breakers being the victors.

Now he's here and Aiden is too and Kailey's behind him and—

My family's all together.

"Come on, Bambi," Smitty says, drawing back and nodding at Jackson.

"Rude."

He tugs at my ponytail. "Stop trying to make trouble. It's beyond time we teach you how to skate."

I gulp. "But you're visiting and the kids want to see you."

There already clambering around the edges, inching toward our gathering.

"I'll just—"

But it's Aiden who surprises me, stepping close, taking an arm, nodding at Smitty to grab the other.

I squeak as I'm lifted into the air then again as my skates hit the ice...and immediately try to slip out from under me.

"Shit," I hiss, clenching at Aiden's arm.

"We've got you."

And, although it takes me a minute, I realize they *do* have me. Aiden and Smitty each holding me beneath an arm, Jackson maneuvering in front of me, his big hands wrapped around mine as he skates backward.

A four-person crew—three of them with professional skating experience, one pathetically resembling Bambi—skating around an ice rink.

It's ridiculous and embarrassing and...

It's my family having my back.

Even though it looks different.

Even though we're spread out across the country.

It's—

I squeal again as I lose my footing, somehow managing to take both Smitty and Aiden out, their big bodies hitting the ice with a sickening *thunk*.

Jackson moves in a flash, drawing me against him, holding me off the surface of the rink, keeping us both steady when I would have gone down with the rest of the ship.

"Umm," I whisper.

Smitty and Aiden are already back on their feet, wincing as they brush snow from their pants.

"Sorry?" I tell them.

Jackson chuckles. "Taking out the competition?"

Smitty scowls, but his eyes are dancing. "Jesus, Bambi."

Aiden just shakes his head at me. "You said it was hopeless." A beleaguered sigh. "I should have believed you."

"Nah, man," Smitty says. "Bambi almost had it."

"That nickname has to go."

"Only one way to make that happen—learn how to skare." His eyes fix me in place. "Now, it's time to go again."

"Yeah, no thanks," I say, shaking my head vehemently. "One near brush with death is enough for the day."

"Practice makes perfect."

"I'll practice making perfect with the hot cocoa dispenser."

Smitty crosses his arms.

I cross them right back—or one of them, anyway. Because I'm clinging to Jackson with the other.

"What do we say?" he asks softly.

And...I melt.

And...I *sigh*.

Because I can't resist that soft voice, the gentle hold.

It coaxes me into another try, and surprises of all surprises, I manage to make it a full lap.

And then another, this time without the side of taking out hockey players.

And then one final one, just holding Jackson's hand as we skate side by side.

"Right," he says as his phone beeps, signaling a low blood sugar.

"Right what?" I ask, already carefully turning us for the exit.

"*Now* it's time for that hot chocolate."

I grin, but then I see him nod to toward his parents, to his mom who's holding her phone up, showing us his number, to his dad who's showing us the steaming pair of hot chocolates.

Always paying attention.

Always watching out for the small details—just like their son.

And I know that I'm lucky my family now includes Kelly and Glen too.

Just like I know as Gran settles next to me, bundled up in a thick puffer coat and a fuzzy hat, that while my family may not always remain the same, it's always growing and changing.

Becoming more.

Becoming somehow even more special.

Because it's mine.

———

Aiden

I wake up to a heavy knock on my condo's front door and glare blearily at my phone in the charger.

"Two in the fucking morning," I mutter, grabbing a pillow

and clamping it over my ears. "It's two o'clock in the morning on my fucking birthday, and I have to deal with this shit."

This shit being my neighbors.

It's not the first time they've pounded drunk on my door, desperate for their roommate to let them in to what they think is their apartment.

This was sort of funny the first time.

I remember those days, drinking too much, being dumb.

But after the second and the third—where I gained status into the inner circle and a code to the keypad to their apartment door—it was no longer cute.

Now, six months later and countless times of bailing them out, I'm *so* not in the mood.

Especially when it's my fucking birthday.

The knocking cuts off and I think—*pray*—that they've gotten the hint.

But it's approximately two seconds later when it starts up again.

I glance at my phone again, see that really five minutes have passed, making it two-seventeen and officially my birthday.

Some present.

I could try to ignore it—but that just means extending the torture. Sighing, I toss back the blankets and stomp to my apartment door, whipping it open to reveal a slender brunette on my doorstep.

"Ho, mama," she says, gaze taking a slow perusal down my body.

"Who the fuck are you?"

"It's me. Luna."

I stare at her, uncomprehendingly.

"From Rockfield?" she adds.

Recognition begins to dawn. "Luna Maybelle?"

"Yup! That's me." She nods, grinning, and I see it then, the glimpse of my best friend from the childhood rink I grew up playing at come out in her smile. Mischief and life. Joy and hard work.

Summers spent spending every spare moment together—her figure skating, me playing hockey.

But she's not little Luna anymore.

Christ, she's anything but—tall, beautiful, curves for days —and she's staring at me.

Because I'm staring at her.

Fucking hell.

I spur myself into motion.

"Luna! Oh my God!" I pull her into a hug. "What the hell are you doing here?"

"It's your birthday!" She holds up a piece of paper that looks faintly familiar. "And, well, it's mine too, remember?"

That's right.

We have the same birthday.

"We're both twenty-five, single, and—"

My eyes narrow in on the paper. It's crumpled and stained, as though it's years old.

A purple and pink swirl decorates the edges and suddenly I remember her painstakingly drawing it as we sat side-by-side at one of the high top tables of the ice rink, waiting for the Zamboni to finish cutting the ice.

Her brow had been furrowed. Her movements carefully controlled.

And I had been obsessing over how pink her lips were and what her butt looked like in her skating dress, so much so that I barely remember what we'd been drawing.

No, I think hard, grabbing on to those memories, not what we'd been *drawing*.

The contract we'd put together.

The contract my hormonal twelve-year-old self had signed.

With a sparkly pink colored pencil.

A giant boulder settles in my stomach, but before I can snap myself out of the horror of those memories, she shoves the paper in my hands then throws her arms around my neck.

"We're getting married!"

THANK YOU FOR READING! I hope you loved Jackson and Claire's story as much as I did! If you want to know what happens to Smitty and Aiden, pick up book one in the Grizzlies Hockey series, 22. **I signed the contract. I just didn't expect her to show up ten years later, ready to cash it in.**

CLICK HERE TO READ 22 NOW>

HAVE YOU MET LAKE JORDAN, **star forward for the Sierra, wedding officiant extraordinaire, and the man everyone hates to play against, and the woman who steals her way into his grumpy, broody heart?** Lake and Nova's book, OVER THE LINE, is available now!

CLICK HERE TO GET OVER THE LINE NOW>

And don't miss my brand new hockey romance, BROKEN LACES. **I'm in love with the owner's daughter. But I can't have her…because if I do I'll lose everything.**
CLICK HERE TO READ BROKEN LACES NOW>

IF YOU ENJOY MY SERIES, considering supporting me on PATREON! Get access to early releases, bonus content, character art, audiobooks, special edition covers, swag, and much more!

CLICK HERE TO SUPPORT ME>

———

Hate missing Elise's new releases? Love contests, exclusive excerpts and giveaways?
Then signup for Elise's newsletter here!
www.elisefaber.com/newsletter

———

If you enjoy my series, considering supporting me on PATREON! Get access to early releases, bonus content, character art, audiobooks, and much more!
CLICK HERE TO SUPPORT ME>

———

And join Elise's fan group, the Fabinators (https://www.facebook.com/groups/fabinators) for insider information, sneak peaks at new releases, and fun freebies! Hope to see you there!

———

BREAKERS HOCKEY SERIES

ALSO BY ELISE FABER

Lace 'em Up

Billionaire's Club (**all stand alone**)

Bad Night Stand

Bad Breakup

Bad Husband

Bad Hookup

Bad Divorce

Bad Fiancé

Bad Boyfriend

Bad Blind Date

Bad Wedding

Bad Engagement

Bad Bridesmaid

Bad Swipe

Bad Girlfriend

Bad Best Friend

Bad Rebound

Bad Romance

Bad Business

Bad Billionaire's Quickies

Love, Action, Camera (all stand alone)

Dotted Line

Action Shot

Close-Up

End Scene

Meet Cute

Love After Midnight (**all stand alone**)

Rum And Notes

Virgin Daiquiri

On The Rocks

Sex On The Seats

Life Sucks Series

Train Wreck

Hot Mess

Dumpster Fire

Clusterf*@k

FUBAR

Perfect Storm

Free Fall

Lost Cause

Roosevelt Ranch Series **(all stand alone, series complete)**

Disaster at Roosevelt Ranch

Heartbreak at Roosevelt Ranch

Collision at Roosevelt Ranch

Regret at Roosevelt Ranch

Desire at Roosevelt Ranch

Phoenix Series **(read in order)**

Phoenix Rising

Dark Phoenix

Phoenix Freed

Phoenix: LexTal Chronicles **(rereleasing soon, stand alone, Phoenix world)**

From Ashes

In Flames

To Smoke

ABOUT THE AUTHOR

USA Today bestselling author, Elise Faber, loves chocolate, Star Wars, Harry Potter, and hockey (the order depending on the day and how well her team -- the Sharks! -- are playing). She and her husband also play as much hockey as they can squeeze into their schedules, so much so that their typical date night is spent on the ice. Elise is the mom to two exuberant boys and lives in Northern California. Connect with her in her Facebook group, the Fabinators or find more information about her books at www.elisefaber.com.

f facebook.com/elisefaberauthor

a amazon.com/author/elisefaber

BB bookbub.com/profile/elise-faber

O instagram.com/elisefaber

d tiktok.com/@elisefaberauthor

g goodreads.com/elisefaber